"Imagine waking up during the witching hour in the '80s and finding a raunchy horror movie on the TV. For a while you're not entirely convinced it's not a snuff video, or a psychedelic nightmare. You feel filthy and reach for the remote to switch it off. But your morbid curiosity forces you to keep going. *Feed the Sky* is that movie."
Robert Weaver, author of *Blessed Skeletons* and *Five Suns Over Somerset*

"*Feed the Sky* is dark and grisly and cosmic in its horror ... and it's also a hell of a lot of fun from start to finish!"
Mark Allan Gunnells, author of *Lucid* and *When it Rains*

"Vile, disturbing, horrifying and down-right traumatizing. Clearly the work of a depraved individual. It's fucked and I loved it."
Horror Oasis Reviews

"Add a dash of *Cabin in the Woods*, a sprinkle of Clive Barker, and a little Edward Lee for good measure, and you get the barest glimpse of what to expect in *Feed the Sky*. Wesley Winters' extreme horror novella will leave even the most seasoned horror reader trembling at the prospect of what waits in the woods."
Brennan LaFaro, author of *I Will Always Find You* and *Noose*

"...truly fucked...very out of control and unpredictable..."
Kristina Osborn, Truborn Press

"A brutal and bloody backwoods bacchanal..."
Christopher Robertson, author of *The Cotton Candy Massacre*

"...a visceral, mind-bending journey...[Winters] cranks the weirdness up to eleven, crafting an unsettling atmosphere that feels as alive as its haunted forests...the narrative twists through layers of cosmic horror, cult rituals, and trippy, character-driven arcs...the imagery is a standout...Winters' characters are raw and real, navigating guilt, desire, and survival instincts in increasingly surreal situations. The chaotic dynamics within the group camping trip—particularly the messy blend of humor and dread—help ground the escalating madness...[Winters] pushes the boundaries of conventional horror to deliver a wholly unique experience—one that shocks, mesmerizes, and haunts. The vivid prose and daring storytelling demand your attention and trust, rewarding readers with an unforgettable descent into a universe where even the sky hungers."
Miguel Gonçalves, author of *The Scarecrow Man* and *School's Night Out*

"...get ready for a lot of blood, bonking, and bodies galore..."
Luc Dantes, contributor to Ghost Watch, *Twisted Horrors*, and *Dark Descent*

ALSO BY WESLEY WINTERS

COLLECTIONS
Nobody's Savior
From the Flood
There Was Always Violence
Documenting Dreadful Existences (Volumes 1-3)
Horrific Holidays
Sickness is in Season

THE TELIGA CITY BLUES
Going Sideways (featured in *The Toll Comes Due*)

THE COSMIC DEVOURER OF LIFE
Feed the Sky (The Fucked Trilogy, Book 1)

THE CRIMSON HIGHNESS
Cave Drawings (featured in *Nobody's Savior*)

SHIFTY THINGS
The Descent of Shadows (Book 0)
Acres of Darkness (Book 1)

ABOVE & BELOW
A Call to Feast (Part 1)
Widespread Terror (Part 2)

OUTSIDE APPEARANCES
That Old House: The Bathroom (Part 2)
HorrorScope: A Zodiac Anthology (Volume 2)
Terrible Lizards
Cursed Cooking
Twisted Horrors
Rise Above
Wild Violence (as Aiden Merchant)
Pulp Harvest (as Aiden Merchant)
Slice of Paradise (as Aiden Merchant)
Blackberry Blood (editing as Aiden Merchant)
Black Dogs, Black Tales (editing as Aiden Merchant)

WESLEY WINTERS

FEED THE SKY

THE FUCKED TRILOGY
— BOOK 1 —

A WINTRY MONSTERS PRESS TITLE

This book is a work of fiction. Names, characters, places, and incidents are products of the author's imagination or are used fictitiously. Any resemblance to actual events or locals or persons, living or dead or the living undead, is entirely coincidental.

Feed the Sky © 2022 by Wesley Winters
Cave Drawings © 2024 by Wesley Winters

All rights reserved, including the right to reproduce the book or portions thereof in any form whatsoever.

For licensing and rights, such as those related to film, contact wintrymonsterspress@gmail.com.

Wintry Monsters Press – An Independent Press and Digital Magazine
Official Website: www.wintrymonsterspress.com

Follow the author on Substack and Instagram: @thewinterseye

First (Gaast) Paperback Edition
ISBN: 9798291040058
Second Text Edition

Cover design by Vlad Gaast
Instagram @v_gaast
Portfolio: industriacriativa.pt/rafael-sales
ArtStation.com/rsales

Feed the Sky was first published in February 2025
"Cave Drawings" first appeared in *Nobody's Savior*, May 2024
—Slashic Horror Press

Refer to www.wintrymonsterspress.com/content-warnings for advisories.

TABLE OF CONTENTS

Prologue ... 1
Sucked dry to feed the sky.

Chapter One ... 12
Camping is all the rage, they say.

Chapter Two ... 22
Things always go wrong when the group separates.

Chapter Three ... 36
We interrupt your sexy time with this important announcement.

Chapter Four ... 48
Impossible things and swallowing darkness.

Chapter Five ... 60
The White Ritual, as performed by the Crimson Highness.

Chapter Six ... 71
A stowaway reveals herself to the "One" that can defeat Him.

Chapter Seven ... 87
Protecting the Order and Lord.

Chapter Eight ... 99
Taking shit to the parking lot. (A finale)

Epilogue ... 104
The mountain swallows deep.

Bonus Content

Author's Sketch Gallery ... 113

Early Renditions of the Gaast Cover Spread ... 125

Cave Drawings (A Prelude Novelette from the *Crimson Highness* series) ... 131

INTRODUCTION

Sometime in 2021, I decided I wanted to try bizarro horror. I even created the pseudonym of Wesley Winters for that original purpose. What's funny is I was influenced by books on my shelf I have not yet read at the time of this book's initial publication. But I love their covers and the idea of blending absurdity into my fiction, so I sat down to specifically write something weird (and maybe even a little off-putting at times).

Feed the Sky didn't end up as bizarro as I thought it would, but it is still the wildest and most out-there story I've ever written. I went out of my way to think of exaggerated and gory things to include, like the [REDACTED] and the [REDACTED] scenes. Upon reading the first draft of *Feed the Sky*, I realized it played out like a campy '80s slasher flick accompanied by a variety of monsters and monstrous sights. And I liked that.

Years have passed since I thought this book would be published. There were two or three presses I thought were going to use it that went on to close their doors and vanish quite suddenly and without warning. After these setbacks, *Feed the Sky* was shelved, though I thought of it often. Occasionally, I returned to the manuscript for new edits, thinking I might publish it myself right away. I even requested some author blurbs around that time, which are included at the front of this book. Despite having early readers praising the story, I ended up not releasing it at that time. For a variety of reasons—one being I decided to work on its prequel series—I continued to postpone *Feed the Sky* from there.

Then, around the summer or fall of 2023, I began working on new stories for a collection that would become *Nobody's Savior*. I wrote and included a short novella called *Cave Drawings*, which acts as a prequel to *Feed the Sky*. At this point, I currently have several others started and stopped. Writing *Cave Drawings* helped reignite my spark for this initial trilogy, and I returned to it in a big way. For months, I outlined mythos for the cult and the Eye of Eyes. I also finished several of the other prequel novellas, and drafted a list of additional books that would eventually accompany them. The finished stories were written out of order, which is why nothing has been released yet. I went back and forth about releasing them before *Feed the Sky* but decided this trilogy had waited long enough to launch. So the prequel series will follow this book instead of preceding it.

Upon returning to *Feed the Sky* (for what felt like the hundredth time), I went back to add in details that would connect it to the rest of the universe I've been outlining. There are many small things mentioned in passing that hold more weight elsewhere now. The story has not changed, however. The prologue was extended a few pages since my early readers reviewed it, but nothing else. I've just edited it many times. Fixed some names. Added some important scars. Small things that would go unnoticed by most upon a reread. But small *important* things, nonetheless.

What you have now is a wild cosmic-horror story that is *meant* to be campy and fun. Even nostalgic. So, don't take it too seriously or you won't enjoy it. That being said, the rest of the series is far more grounded by comparison. But I clearly went off the rails writing this one, and that was purposeful.

I also want to emphasize you should read the bonus content I've included here because all of it expands upon things in and around this story. Before *The Fucked* trilogy has ended, many, many more people will die. If you're a fan of high body counts, then you've found the right series to enjoy.

Wesley Winters
February 1, 2025

PROLOGUE

Sucked Dry to Feed the Sky

June 2011

They've been running for five minutes, maybe longer. Dennis can't believe the horrors they've just witnessed here in the mountains surrounding town. His daughter, Farrah, isn't trying to make sense of it; she didn't see everything her father did because she'd been some distance behind him when he suddenly turned to run. Now, she's just looking for a way back to their car. This wasn't a trip she ever wanted to attend in the first place, but her mother made her. Two weeks in fuckin' Tennessee, away from home and all her friends during the height of summer vacation. It was all such bullshit.

Bond with your father, Kate had told her. *You two fight too much.*

A lot of good it's doing her. After just one night in the wilderness looking for truffles, they are already in trouble. With whom, she is not sure. They *looked* like moving trees, but that was probably just some weird camouflage suit a poacher purchased. She'd heard of them wearing sasquatch costumes as well; why not dress as trees to get the drop on someone? People are crazy, especially isolated mountain people. Maybe they'd stumbled upon a hidden pot farm. It's not like her father has yet to offer an explanation as to why they are running like hell.

"Come on!" Dennis commands breathlessly, keeping the lead.

Farrah is working her legs as hard as she can, but she doesn't have her father's stride. "You're faster than me!"

"Keep up! You're too far behind!"

No, shit, she thinks, out of breath. *You're not even trying to keep sight of me. As usual.*

Farrah feels something snag her ankle and she goes down hard. Dirt kicks up into her face and temporarily blinds her. She cries as she rubs vigorously at her eyes, the grit collecting around her eyelids. It sounds like her father is still running, unaware or without concern for her wellbeing. When he yells next, he sounds much farther ahead of her than before: "I see a clearing!"

Farrah collects herself from the ground, kicks away the vines that tripped her, and continues to rub her eyes. They sting and clearly need to be flushed. She retrieves the bottle attached to her hip and begins pouring water over her dirtied face at an angle. It takes some effort, but she manages to rinse her eyes enough to continue. Most of the bottle is now empty, though, which can't be good if they're lost.

In the distance, her father suddenly begins to scream as if he's being flayed. Farrah's heart leaps into her throat and she freezes. When the screaming comes accompanied by pleas for help, she finds herself moving once more. First, a deliberate walk. Then a run. She dashes through the trees, discovers a strange clearing, and skids to a halt.

Her father is levitating in place with a visible patch of sky overheard. Farrah scans the surrounding area and notices several other similar views of moonlight and stars casting upon the dirt and leaves, amidst the mostly clustered treetops. She turns back to her father to ask him where they are but realizes something is happening to him as he floats rigidly in the air.

Dennis's face has started peeling into small strips that are lifting into the night sky, as if carried by a controlled breeze. His eyes are bloodshot and his nose is bleeding. Crimson beads are dripping down his lips and leaping away from his mouth to feed the stars next. Moisture from his forehead is following suit; it appears that Dennis is being slowly juiced by invisible hands.

"Get me down from here!" he screams, his arms stuck against his sides and his spine arched painfully. He wiggles his fingers and twitches his ankles but can barely move himself otherwise.

Farrah approaches several feet but remains a presumably safe distance away. There's a circular swath of light below her father's feet, perhaps three feet in diameter, like a grounded halo or marker. Farrah assumes crossing this border will land her in a similar predicament, which she would like to avoid.

"Can you reach out and grab anything?" she asks, knowing the answer.

Dennis roars, "WHAT THE FUCK DO YOU THINK, FARRAH? I'VE JUST FORGOTTEN I HAVE GODDAMN ARMS OR SOMETHIN? PULL ME DOWN!" A large strip of his cheek peels away from his face and rises toward the treetops, leaving behind a band of red that brings tears to his eyes. His fingers continue to curl and flex in pain but he's still unable to move in any way that is helpful. "Please," he whimpers. "Hurry!"

Farrah looks for a stick, finds one, and uses it to poke her father. Despite passing into the light, nothing happens. She expected the stick to be torn from her hand, but she doesn't feel a tug of any sort. She tries using it to push her father closer to the edge of the beam, but it snaps in half. He doesn't move so much as a centimeter in the process. Something has a firm hold on him.

"What are you doing? Just grab my hand and pull!"

"I'm not getting stuck like you!" she screams back, her panic rising. "I need a thicker stick. I need a *branch*. Hold on!"

Farrah turns from the clearing and hurries back into the trees to find something stronger. A moment later, she's found what she's looking for and returns to her father's side. His back seems to have somehow arched even more, causing his shirt to lift several inches and reveal his belly. The skin there is starting to peel as well, now that it has been exposed to the skylight. Her father's tears are immediately evaporating into the air as they fall from his eyes.

"DO SOMETHING, GOD DAMN IT!"

Farrah holds the branch like a lance and charges at her father, slamming hard into his side. Dennis howls in pain but doesn't budge. The resistance causes Farrah to lose her grip on the branch and tumble forward in an awkward spin. Her arm breaks the border momentarily, but she quickly pulls herself back into the darkness and rolls several feet away. She checks herself and finds no injury. She won't take that risk again. As far as she's concerned, her failed attempts have proven her father cannot be saved.

He's fucked.

"Stop fooling around, Farrah!"

She stands and rounds the circle to view her father from the front. Though she doesn't like him, she does love him. Somewhere in the past, they used to get along. They used to play for hours with her dolls and plastic food. He used to tuck her into bed and cuddle her until she fell asleep. There was a past she did not want to forget. She begins to cry because she knows tonight, she'll lose him forever.

"Don't do that," he says, crying as well. "You can get me out of this."

She shakes her head. "I can't," she sobs. "If slamming into you didn't make any difference, nothing I do is going to help." She reaches into her back pocket and retrieves her phone in a last-ditch effort. She holds it over her head and walks back and forth across the clearing, searching for a signal. But she can't find anything better than the dreaded X.

Her father's eyes search the treetops as he blinks back his tears. He licks his lips, tastes the streaks of blood there, and says a panicked prayer beneath his breath.

"Daddy?"

His eyes drop to view her as best he can, because he cannot move his head; his chin is being yanked upward by the invisible force keeping him in place several feet above the forest floor.

"Yes?" he says.

"What should I do?"

Dennis remembers the pistol strapped to his calf, the pistol he brought in case anyone tried to fuck with them for their truffles. Tweekers often scoured the woods for such rarities. There were mushrooms and roots and...

"Daddy?"

He snaps back to reality—the one that intends to leave his daughter defenseless atop a fucking mountain in the middle of the night—and tries looking at her once more. "My gun," he says. "Can you get it?"

Farrah looks at the strap against his calf. It's snapped shut, locking the gun in place. And yet, with the branch, she might be able to free it.

"Why do you—"

"Because I want you to use it," he says, interrupting her. "On me. This...fucking *hurts*. The moonlight or the stars or the fucking sky—I don't know—but it's fuckin' draining me or something. I feel weak and light and...so goddamn *parched*."

Farrah eyes her father's belly and realizes it appears to have shrunken, however slightly, as if her father is losing weight right before her eyes. Wherever there's skin visible, she can see Dennis has peeled and is continuing to do so. Moisture from his mouth is visibly lifting from his face and floating above them as they speak.

Dennis is right; he's being sucked dry.

"Are you sure?" Farrah asks, referring to the gun. Her tears are coming harder now, soaking her cheeks in the darkness where she safely stands.

Dennis squeezes his eyes tightly and tries to nod but the force won't allow him. "Yes, honey," he croaks after a hard minute of trying to swallow. His throat is incredibly raw already. "I just want this to be quick."

Farrah picks up the tree branch once more and uses it to pop the snap of her father's holster. She then rams the muzzle from below repeatedly until she's freed the weapon from his leg. It falls to the ground and waits. Farrah stands frozen for a long minute, scared to retrieve the weapon.

Before she can bring herself to move and finally collect it, her father speaks:

"I love you, pumpkin. I'm so sorry we haven't been good together these last few years. I want you to know you've grown into a beautiful woman, and you'll make someone so happy one day. I just wish I could be around to see it."

Crying loudly now, Farrah uses the branch to scoop the revolver out of the light and pick it up. She then disengages the safety and takes aim at her father's temple. "I love you too, Daddy. If the sky's gonna take you, it better leave your eyes to watch over me."

She pulls the trigger. Her father's head should snap to the opposite side, but the sky's unnatural grasp on his frame only allows him to shudder from the impact. The other side of his skull still explodes, though; but rather than pepper the forest floor with bloody fragments of bone patched with hair, the pieces are sucked upward into the halo where they rise toward the night sky.

Farrah falls to her knees and screams until her voice breaks. As she gasps for breath, choking, she tosses the pistol away from her. She never wants to see or touch it again.

Several minutes pass with her lying in the dirt, shaking. Then she hears voices approaching the clearing, and quickly gathers herself up to hide in the brush. Maybe it's the men dressed as trees, looking to see if their trap worked on her father.

No, she tells herself as she wipes her face with the bottom of her shirt. *They didn't do this. This isn't man-made. This is impossible.*

The voices are getting close enough now that she can hear some of what they're saying.

"...in four more nights..."

"...if she comes? What will we..."

"...I've waited long enough for the Ground Lord to..."

"...but what if she..."

"Quiet, my love. We can handle her..."

"...and the Lord?"

"We can guide Him."

"Look, Your Highness."

Two women in crimson cloaks step into the clearing from the far side of Farrah's location. Because of their hoods, much of their features are hidden, even as they near the moonlit halo that has taken her father's life. The women stop outside the circle and inspect his corpse for several moments in silence. One of the women begins to smile as she rounds the death circle for a complete view of their captive. "This is good," she says. "The eyes will need all the sustenance they can get."

"He wasn't alone, Your Highness," the other woman tells her, turning her head toward the ground where Farrah abandoned her father's pistol.

The leader follows the woman's gaze and nods. "If anyone remains on the mountain, they'll find another one of my traps soon enough." She pulls back her hood and reveals a shining mane of red hair. All along her neck are angry, seeping cuts. She takes the other woman in her hands and stands close to her. "I've spilled a lot of blood for this White Ritual. We won't fail again." The women kiss deeply. When the leader pulls away, her companion shudders for air.

"Yes, your Highness," she says. "But what of your premonition? The girl?"

"There is no mortal that could survive this mountain with us. We've made sure of it. Now gather the Others.

There are more preparations yet to be made."

The leader turns away from the clearing and returns to the cover of the forest. The other robed woman follows after taking one final, suspicious look around the clearing. Farrah ducks down to keep out of sight and waits for her to leave. Once both women are out of sight, she counts to sixty before standing from the brush. Slowly, she approaches her father's pistol and considers picking it up. But the closer she comes to it, the harder her body shakes. Images of her father's exploding temple replay in her head, making her sick. She fights back tears and turns away from the weapon to look toward the trees.

Where does she go now? What does she do?

For hours, she wanders in a direction different from the women. She doesn't want to cross their path again. They knew of the halos and the trees. They are somehow part of this. Farrah can't make sense of it all, though. They can't just be territorial pot farmers. The redheaded one spoke of traps and something about eyes. Clearly, she is crazy. And with those robes—are they part of some sort of cult hiding up in these mountains?

Farrah is nearly depleted of energy when she stumbles into a hole and lands hard on her face several feet down inside a sloped entrance she never saw coming. At first, she remains still, too scared to move. But then she lifts her face from the dirt and looks ahead of herself. She's fallen into the opening of what appears to be a cave, she thinks, as she stands unsteadily upon her tired feet. The space is dark but not unused; she sees unlit candles and folded clothing and...

Bones?

She reaches into her back pocket and retrieves her phone to illuminate the cave.

In the center of the space, there's an altar built of wooden logs and slabs. It's about three feet tall and as large as a small dinner table. Beneath it is a pile of bones, mostly splintered and broken, but containing at least two skulls visible in the heap.

Farrah swallows and turns from the altar. Along the walls of the cave are makeshift beds of blankets and pillows, divided by candles and food rations, or what remains of them. There's trash scattered about, including wrappers for protein bars and crackers. A pack of bottled water rests against the back wall next to a crumpled wad of cash.

What the hell is this place? she wonders.

Drawn and painted along the walls and ceiling are shapes that appear to make up a language unfamiliar to her. There are also eyes, dozens of them, scattered in the midst of the writing that brings to Farrah's mind hieroglyphics.

A shiver chases down her spine, and she shuts her eyes. She wants to leave. There's something strange about these people. How many of them are there? If they aren't occupying this cave currently, then where have they set up camp?

She climbs back out into the forest a minute later, shaken and dirty. When she looks to the sky, she sees a plume of smoke rising from the north.

She feels compelled to discover its source and learn more about the redheaded woman's plans. These people killed her father for a reason. To feed something, to give it power. Didn't she mention a Ground Lord? Whatever that is. One of them said it, she thinks.

Farrah swallows back her tears and decides she must

bury her pain, lock it away someplace in the back of her mind where it cannot slow her down.

She must make this woman pay for what she's done.

CHAPTER 1

CAMPING IS ALL THE RAGE THEY SAY

Four Days Later

"If we get separated, we have these to signal our location."

Justin shows the group a small collection of flare guns resting atop the contents of his pack. Tommy snatches one from the bag and turns it in his hands.

"What would happen if I shot you with this?" he asks, grinning stupidly.

"I don't know. But don't do it."

"Would you catch fire?"

"Maybe."

"Cool."

Justin yanks the gun from his younger brother's hand and shoves it back into his pack. "You idiots need to be better prepared for this trip. We're about to get fucked out of our minds on mushrooms and you don't seem at all worried about our safety."

Tommy snorts into laughter. "Dude, you need to relax. Stop acting like Mom."

The others nod in agreement. In all, there's five of them attending the trip. There are the Market brothers, of course, Justin and Tommy. There's also Julie, Tommy's latest girlfriend; Adam, his best friend; and Mary, the girl from down the street whose parents are tight with the Markets. She's only nineteen, making her the youngest in the group by several years. Justin isn't thrilled to have her tagging along, but his parents insisted she be included. Mary's parents apparently begged them, though he isn't sure why. He doesn't think they would have pushed for it had they known the group would be intoxicated most of the trip.

"When do we leave?" Adam asks with a heavy sigh.

"Now, if you're all ready," Justin says, throwing his pack into the back of his parents' Escalade alongside the others. The vehicle is overcrowded with things and uncomfortable, but they won't be driving for very long. The parking area Justin has chosen for them is only twenty minutes away, in Arwyn. He's camped in the general area before, but it's been a few years. The others have never camped in the actual wild, though, so it's up to him to maintain order.

Once everyone has piled into the Escalade, Justin turns on Navigation and locates his sunglasses. Sitting beside him is Adam, who immediately gets to work on their lack of music for the road. In the back, smashed tightly together, is Tommy, Julie, and Mary. Justin's eyes flick to the rearview mirror to where he sees his brother and Julie are already trading saliva. Mary looks awkwardly out the window, trying her best to ignore the inappropriate PDA. Justin feels for her, but there's nothing he can do to stop his brother during the drive.

"Let's hit it," Adam commands, smacking the

dashboard and pointing toward the road. "Onward!"

Justin shakes his head and pulls out of the driveway.

The parking area is unmarked and hardly noticeable from the road. Justin makes his turn onto the gravel and immediately feels the difference beneath them. The lot is located a hundred yards further, nestled amongst the trees and out of sight. There's one other vehicle present when he parks, a yellow sedan that's just as old as he.

"Yikes, take a look at that thing," Adam says, jerking a thumb in its direction.

"Isn't that where you were conceived?" Tommy asks from the back, snickering.

"Julie, control your man."

"He's not much of a man," Justin says, shutting off the engine and throwing open his door.

Tommy flicks him on the back of the neck before he can step outside. "Fuck you."

Mary moves toward the path leading away from the vehicles and says, "How far of a hike is it?"

Justin throws on his largest pack—the one he's going to carry on his back—and passes the cooler to his brother. "I know of a dirt clearing about a mile and a half from here. It's up a sharp incline but has a nice overlook of the town. Should only take us an hour to reach, give or take."

There's a collective groan from the others that Justin chooses to ignore.

Tommy hefts the cooler handed to him and carries it over to where Mary is standing beside a sign noting local radio frequencies in case of an emergency. As he pulls up alongside her, he grins and says, "Shit, this is heavy. You and

I can take turns."

Julie appears next to him and swats her hand across the back of his head. "Stop your flirting, asshole."

Mary chuckles. "I wouldn't have called that flirting. If that was his intention, he's really bad at it."

"Trust me, he is."

The girls laugh and start walking. They each have on their personal packs, which are much smaller than those carried by the Market brothers and Adam. When Tommy takes notice of this, he asks, "Did you ladies even bring camping supplies?"

Mary and Julie pause as Justin continues to unload the vehicle.

"I've got clothes, toiletries, a book, one of those light-up clips for reading in the dark, and...my water bottle," Mary says, trying to remember everything. "What else do I need? Doesn't Justin have the tent?"

Tommy lowers the cooler, laughing, and smacks the top of it for emphasis. "What about your sleeping bag? Or a pillow? Bug spray? A flashlight? Sunscreen?"

Justin shuts the trunk, clicks the lock button on his key fob, and follows Adam to the others. Both he and Adam are carrying various bags on each side of them, along with the large packs strapped to their backs.

Mary is biting her lip as she lets out a heavy sigh.

Julie says, "I'm sharing your shit, Tommy."

"Not my pillow."

"Why the hell not?"

"You think your large head will fit with mine on a regular sized pillow?"

Julie swipes a handful of dirt from the trail and throws it at her boyfriend's face. He shields himself and curses.

"You're such an asshole," she growls.

"If you're stealing my pillow, then I'll be using your tits," he says.

Justin moves beyond the girls, grunting from the weight of everything he's carrying. "Enough, guys. We can fight about this shit once we reach the clearing. But Adam and I have too much in our hands to just stand around. Let's get moving."

By the time they've reached the clearing, everyone is thoroughly exhausted despite having taken several breaks during their hike. Tommy practically tosses the cooler away from him prior to dropping into the dirt. Justin gets immediately to work on the tent while Adam seeks materials for their fire pit. However tempting, they can't stop yet, not so close to nightfall.

"What should we do?" Mary asks. Julie is a step behind her and unhappy to be included in this offer for help.

Justin continues to unpack the tent and says, "You can join Adam in gathering stock from the woods. Or...enjoy the scenery, I guess."

Mary walks beyond him and looks over the mountainside. She can see a portion of the town below, as well as the interstate and the wilderness beyond it. "This is a pretty good view. Have you camped at this spot before?"

"Nope, just passed through."

"I'm surprised nobody is already here using it."

"Honestly, I worried it might be taken. Especially since it's only a mile at most from the cars."

Julie scans the clearing and sighs with exasperation. "I think we need seats. Did you bring any foldout chairs?"

Justin points to where Adam has laid down several thin bags with straps. "There's a few. And I put the others over there," he says, pointing out their locations. "I can't set up everything for you all."

Mary walks up beside him and rests a hand on his shoulder. "We appreciate it, Justin. You're being a stud."

Julie nods in reassurance. "Oh, yeah. Um, thanks."

Justin smiles over his shoulder at Mary. The sun is backlighting her perfectly from this angle. She looks like an angel now, young and vibrant, spiritual and breathtaking. Justin licks the sweat from his lips and returns his attention to the tent materials. Suddenly, he's in need of a distraction.

Tommy pretends to snore loudly from his place in the dirt. Julie kicks him in the hip and says, "Get up and do something!"

Mary looks for Adam and sees him in the trees some fifty yards away. As she leaves to join him, Julie asks where she's going.

"To get firewood and stuff."

Julie considers joining, but instead yanks her boyfriend to his feet. "Help with the tent or you're getting blue balls tonight."

"Um, that should be happening anyway," Justin says, loud enough for all to hear. "This tent may look big, but we are all going to be *pretty* close to one another, especially if some of us are sharing pillows and shit. So, keep it all in your pants. Please. For the love of God."

Tommy laughs as he stands to stretch. "There are woods, Jus. We don't need the tent to have a good time."

"Speak for yourself," Julie grumbles, unfolding a chair and dropping into it.

In the nearby trees, Mary catches up to Adam and asks

what she should be looking for.

"Shit, you scared me," he tells her, dramatically placing a hand over his heart. "Look, it's good you're here. I actually just put down my bundle because of this." He points to a downed tree that has been cut up into three-foot portions by a park ranger or camper. "They may not look all that big, but they're heavy. If we take a few of these logs over to the campsite, we can get a real wilderness vibe going."

"What about the foldout chairs you guys brought?"

"Additional seating is always good. Besides, we can use them as tabletops as well. Put our plates on them and other shit." He lays one flat on its severance and spreads open his hands. "See? A makeshift table!"

Mary laughs and nods, convinced. "Alright, let's do it."

As they drop the first log near the tent-in-progress, Justin says, "What's that for?"

This time it's Mary to lay the log flat as a proposal. "If not to sit on, then to eat on."

"Good thinking, Mary."

"Don't smile at her," Adam jokes. "It was *my* idea. Smile at me, bitch."

Justin turns his smile into a sarcastic grin as he looks toward Adam instead.

"That's...better," Adam mumbles, turning away.

Justin drops the grin and claps his hands together in Adam's face. "Enough of this tomfoolery. Get back to work! The lot of you!" He chuckles and returns to the tent. Adam shoves him forward from behind and quickly flees the scene. Mary watches this exchange with amusement and catches Justin's eye. Embarrassed, he breaks the connection and turns away.

"Hey, did you hear about those guys that robbed the drugstore and stole all the Viagra?"

The group turns to eye Tommy, some with beers pressed to their lips.

"Well, the cops had to put out an alert for two *hardened* criminals," he said, smiling.

Mary laughs into her drink and sprays the fire. The others roll their eyes, having expected as much from Tommy.

"At least one of you understands a good joke when they hear it," he says, taking a long pull from his beer.

Mary cleans herself off with Adam's help. Justin watches from the corner of his eye, annoyed that he even cares. Tommy takes notice and tells his brother to walk with him a moment.

"Do my eyes deceive me?" he jokes once they're out of earshot of the others.

Justin turns back to the glow of their campsite and the stars shining overhead. It's a clear night with a beautiful view of the sky. He thinks as much and is relieved with the luck he's had with planning the trip so far.

"Justin?"

"Hmm?"

"Are you listening?"

Justin looks to his brother and follows him deeper into the trees. "What did you say?"

"Are you into Mary?"

"Um…I don't know." He laughs a little, shrugging. "I haven't seen her in a while."

"In other words, she's suddenly caught your attention?"

"I suppose."

Tommy shakes his head and says, "I think you have some competition. And I know you've noticed."

"I wouldn't call it competition, seeing as I'm not after her."

"Why not?"

"I don't know. I'm not looking for anything right now."

Tommy stops near the downed tree Adam found earlier and takes a seat on one of its severed logs. "Who says a fun vacation fuck needs to turn into something?"

"I really don't think she's like that."

"Maybe not. But how can you know if you don't talk to her?"

Justin takes a seat as well and runs a hand through his sweat-slicked hair. "Why do you care so much if I try something?"

"I wouldn't say I *care*, but you're a bit wound tight. We're out in the mountains, camping, and drinking, and... Hell, why shouldn't you be fucking?"

Justin laughs at his brother's stupidity and thinks about it. He's twenty-seven with a good job and a nice apartment. He lives alone, eats alone, sleeps alone. In his free time, he exercises and takes hikes through the woods. Though Justin isn't necessarily lonely, he does feel a pinch some days. A pinch that says something is missing. Or someone.

"What's going on up there?" Tommy asks, pressing his finger into the side of his brother's head with unnecessary force.

Justin smacks his finger away and says, "Look, I'll talk to her. But I'm not looking to just fuck in the woods like you and Julie."

"Speaking of," Tommy says, jumping to his feet, "let's dig out some of those shrooms and get this party started!"

Back at the campsite, Adam talks to Mary from their side of the fire. Julie looks for Tommy but can't see him through the surrounding darkness. She's alone and bored and ignored, unlike the younger girl in their group. So, she retrieves her cell phone and tries browsing Instagram. When the home feed fails to load after an insufferable minute, Julie grumbles and tries another one of her apps. Again, there's nothing to see. She eyes the signal status of her phone and sees that the bars are nonexistent. Though she wants to smash the device in frustration, she tries restarting it instead. Just in case that will somehow fix her problem.

From beyond the clearing overlooking Arwyn, a figure inches through the brush to spy on the campsite and the treats it has to offer.

CHAPTER 2

THINGS ALWAYS GO WRONG WITH THE GROUP SEPARATES

Mary likes Justin, has since she was ten and he was graduating from high school. Sometimes, the Markets would send Justin or Tommy over to babysit her or take her to the movies. It was during these nights that the parents got together without their kids in the way. Though Justin would sometimes ditch Mary someplace to go do his own thing, she spent enough time with him over the years to develop a crush. Then she turned fourteen and her parents started sending her out on her own. Justin was no longer around at the Market house and Tommy was eighteen by then. Though she liked Tommy just fine, he'd always been the immature brother. Justin, on the other hand, was intelligent and capable and...well, he was handsome. She couldn't forget that.

Adam seems nice, too—she tells herself as they talk by

the fire—but he's not Justin. The truth is her parents couldn't care less if she was invited on the camping trip or not. She'd skipped them entirely and asked Gemma Market on the sidewalk one day about it. She'd led their conversation to the trip and how fun it sounded. Gemma had fallen for the act and said she'd ask the boys to give her a call for old time's sake. Mary is right where she wants to be, right where she planned to be. With Justin sitting several feet away from her with a beer in hand.

The game is already afoot.

Justin hands the baggy over to his brother before cracking open another drink. Tommy holds the mushrooms above their heads and howls for attention. "Eyes over here, folks! I got the goods you've been waiting for! So, open those mouths and drop your pants!"

Adam stops talking with Mary and turns to look. Without his focused attention, Mary feels like she can finally release an anxious breath. Her mind immediately wanders as she scans the campground, what little she can see of it in the dark. On the other side of the tent, she hears rustling in the bushes but no one else reacts. She waits several beats for more but there's nothing. Perhaps she's just heard a raccoon or possum.

"Here," Adams says, passing her a mushroom. "Have you done this before?"

Mary eyes the liberty cap and gently presses it between her fingertips. "No. I don't really do drugs."

"They're harmless, really. With friends to look after you, I wouldn't worry."

"Are you sure?"

"It's not like acid. You'll probably hallucinate some, but the effects are mild. Especially if you eat in moderation."

Mary looks beyond Adam to observe the rest of the group. Tommy has already eaten several and has a handful more in his palm. Justin has only grabbed two of the mushrooms from the baggy and is taking his time nibbling on their rubbery texture. Julie has taken her boyfriend's lead and shoved a handful into her mouth already. She is chewing vigorously and taking drinks from her beer to get them down.

"Wow, Tommy and Julie seem to have their eyes on the prize," she says, laughing nervously.

"Look, you're new to it. I would only eat a couple if I were you. But look." He gently touches her chin and moves her face directly before his. "You want to have a good mindset first. If you're scared or upset, the shrooms will amplify that. So, you know, *relax,* and make sure you're looking for fun while eating them."

Mary licks her lips and holds her breath without realizing it. Adam is slightly intoxicating, she notices, but it's Justin she wants. She reinforces that in her mind and moves her head so that Adam's hand drops from her chin. Then she smiles shyly and looks down at the mushroom in her hand once more. "How many are you going to take?" she asks.

"I think I'll do a small handful. That should be about...a medium dose. I would go harder but..."

"But what?"

He catches her eye and says, "I want to be aware enough to help you along. Make sure you're alright."

Mary blushes and looks away, biting her lip. Damn boy was making it hard on her to retain focus. But she hadn't kept her virginity this long to lay with the *friend*. She wanted the top dog.

"Thanks for the help," she whispers, placing the mushroom into her mouth and chewing. It's got a sponginess to it, one she's expected. The taste is earthy, not the sort of flavor she would generally seek out in a meal. She wonders if she should swish it with beer like Julie has several times already.

Beside her, Adam casually chews two at a time, like they're Skittles. He looks over at the others and watches them laugh and make jokes at each other's expense. Justin is the most reserved, but even he looks like he's having fun. Mary tries to keep her mind on happy things, like painting in the garden or skipping rocks at the beach.

Or touching Justin...

She shakes her head and smiles to herself, embarrassed, before tossing another mushroom into her mouth.

She doesn't notice Adam's sideways glance as he admires her beauty, already dead set on her and planning his future moves.

Once the mushrooms start taking hold of the group, Justin leaves the fire to relieve himself. He goes far enough into the woods to be out of sight, then unzips his pants and reaches in. The surrounding woods are quiet, dark, and mysterious. There's a slight chill in the air, but he likes it. As he begins watering the bush in front of him, he tilts his head back to examine the starry sky. The constellations are moving as if alive. They aren't doing anything extraordinary (yet), but their activity is amusing, nevertheless.

Back at the campfire, Tommy and Julie are getting loud and wild. He can hear snorting laughter and people falling over. Before leaving, he noticed Mary keeping close with Adam as her trip began to take effect. He thinks that it should be him guiding her along, not Adam. Adam is just a player, always has been. Sure, he's a nice guy, very caring. But he also jumps from girl to girl like their bowls of candy to sample a few times before moving on.

"Fuck him," he says, looking down at his penis in hand. "Right? Fuck him. She shouldn't fall for his tricks. I've got to keep them separated."

He shakes off and puts himself away. As he turns, something latches onto his ankle, and he falls forward. Annoyed, he grumbles and rolls over to see what has snagged him. There's a thicket of thorns stretching out from the bottom of the wet bush, as if reaching for him. Justin shakes his head, curses some more, and gets to his feet. As he leaves the tree line, he tells himself, "Not today, Satan."

"Goddamn, you should see yourself right now," Tommy says, eyeing Julie with lust. Her breasts have engorged before his very eyes, tearing open the front of her blouse. He knows they're not truly so large, but he doesn't care in the least.

"Why?" she asks him, taking another pull of her beer. "What do I look like?"

"A fucking goddess!" Tommy grabs her by the hand and pulls her to her feet. "Follow me," he says, directing her toward the woods. As they pass his brother, he tells him, "Don't wait up."

"Never do," Justin replies, returning to the fire where Adam and Mary are sitting close together and observing their surroundings with obvious wonder.

Tommy pulls Julie hard behind him, practically rushing

her toward the trees. Julie tells him to relax but he doesn't listen. They dive into the wilderness a moment later and embrace.

"Wait a second," Julie says, smacking him on the chest. "Look up."

He does. The sky above them is glowing orange and red, lighting the forest around them. Grinning widely, Tommy steps deeper into the woods to see more. Though there are many shadows—shadows that seem to move on their own accord—he is not scared. The lighting has left him enchanted and excited. Julie seems to feel the same, because she's twirling now, as if imitating a singing princess in an old school Disney movie.

Tommy laughs as he watches her float through the woods, deeper still. At times, it looks as if she's levitating, getting higher and higher. He claps his hands together and whistles approvingly. "Goddamn, girl—look at you!"

Above them, the sky growls, and splits open. Stars are shoved aside, as are the brilliant colors. A darkness takes precedent, and eyes appear in its center. Large eyes that look down upon them with curious amusement. Eyes that seem to communicate with Tommy, *You did good, my son. Look at her. Just look at her.*

Tommy turns his attention back to Julie and nods in vigorous agreement. *I did*, he thinks. *She's fuckin' wild!*

Julie stops her twirling and calls for him to join her. As he gives chase, she turns and runs away, laughing.

Deeper into the woods they go. Away from the glow of the campsite and the voices of friends and family. Deeper into the trees where evil things are watching and waiting.

Mary feels bubbly and warm inside. She's horny, too, she realizes. Very horny. Adam's touch makes her wet and she tries to fight it, but her body wants him. She occasionally glances toward the tent, considering its private escape. But then there's Justin, the man of her dreams, sitting only five feet away. He's quiet and lonely. She can tell. He steals looks at her from time to time, and it's obvious he wants Adam to leave. Which means he wants her, too, doesn't it?

"Fuck you, Adam," she says aloud without meaning to.

Adam slides a half foot away from her in surprise. "Wh–what? Did I do something wrong?"

Justin watches with interest, his lips sealed.

Like Adam, Mary begins to stutter. "I'm, uh, I'm sorry. I didn't mean to s–say that."

"Did you hallucinate something?" he asks, hopeful.

"Yeah, I think so. You were grabbing me all over," she lies, hating herself a little. Suddenly, the sky isn't so bright and starry anymore. The magic is changing, as is the campsite. The trees on the outside seem larger now. The darkness has thickened like fog, creeping toward the fire. Even Justin seems to be sitting further away, as if he's picked up his chair and relocated a safe distance from them. As for the sky, it's grown angry with swirling clouds.

Mary embraces herself and begins to shake. "Make it stop!"

Hands appear around her shoulders, and she's directed into the tent. At first, she thinks it's Adam, ever helpful. But when she opens her eyes next, she sees it's Justin who has rescued her.

"Where's Adam?" she asks.

"I think he's tripping a bit, as well," Justin tells her as he scoops up a blanket for her to hold against her chest. "You might have scared him," he adds with a laugh.

"What do you mean?"

"He ran off toward the trees."

"Shouldn't someone go after him? Make sure he doesn't get lost?"

Justin passes her a bottled water and says, "I saw him going toward Tommy and Julie's general location. He'll be fine. He just might see more than he bargained for."

Mary takes a drink of the water and feels immediately soothed. The magic is returning, as is the warmth in her belly. "You sure?" she asks.

Justin nods and flicks on a nearby lantern. "This isn't his first rodeo. Far from it. He's safe."

Mary smiles and takes another sip. *This is my chance*, she realizes. *We're all alone and hidden from the others.*

She places a hand on Justin's knee and thanks him for the water. Justin straightens a little and she swears the bulge in his pants increases in size. Or is that just the mushrooms having fun with her? She can't say. For all she knows, this isn't even Justin. Maybe she is hallucinating in a bush somewhere, giggling and petting herself wildly while the others are laughing at her expense.

God, I hope this is real, she thinks, leaning forward and parting her lips.

Adam is angry as he stomps through the woods and slips a little on the curving path. He has no idea where he is right now, nor does he care. What he knows is Justin swooped in and stole his girl right out from under him. Some fucking friend. He knew he should have brought a date on this trip. Two girls to three guys wasn't ever going to work. Not unless Julie got so fucked up on mushrooms and alcohol that she wanted a threesome. He'd heard she was the type, but Tommy had taken her away for himself. So, fat chance that was happening.

"Fucking cock," he growls, kicking a stone into the darkness. "Fuckin' throbbing thing."

Agitated with his swollen condition and solitude, Adam drops his pants and takes matters into his own hands. As he begins stroking himself vigorously, the leaves above him shake with anticipation. He pauses to crane his neck upwards for a look. Though he can't see anything in the overhead branches, he swears there are eyes on him.

"Fuck them," he decides. "Let them watch." He tugs on himself harder. "Enjoy the show, motherfuckers!"

He closes his eyes and imagines Mary on her knees before him. As the minutes tick by without release, he becomes frustrated and stops. He's about to bend down for his pants when he suddenly feels hands sliding up and over his balls.

What the...?

He squints into the darkness and sees a form there, on their knees and level with his cock.

"Mary?"

The form evolves from a shadow into a naked woman; one he does not recognize. She has crimson hair and ruby lipstick amplifying her pouty lips. Her tits are pointed with sharpened nipples. As Adam takes in her beauty, the girl continues to massage his balls, eventually moving one of her hands to the shaft of his cock and working it gently.

"Who are you?" he asks.

The woman smiles wider, impossibly so. The corners of her mouth stretch as high as her eyes, which seem to flash in the darkness. Adam is momentarily startled and pulls back a step. The girl's face returns to normal, and she pulls him closer.

"Relax," she tells him, stroking his cock eagerly. "Let me please you."

Adam nods as his eyes scan the woman's body in the shadows. She has an eye tattooed between her breasts and numerous scars and healing cuts across her entire body, including some that are more recent along her neck and hands. He doesn't know what to make of them, but he hardly cares—the woman's warm mouth has engulfed his cock completely as her fingernails gently rake the underside of his balls. Her nose is pressed against his stomach as he moans. Though it all feels so real, he assumes it's just part of his hallucinatory trip. But that's more than okay, because the rush he is feeling is unlike any of the excitement he's ever had before.

I don't care if she's not really here, he tells himself. *This is fuckin' amazing.*

A voice echoes from inside his head: "I will devour you..."

It didn't belong to the girl with the busy mouth. The voice was deep, like the rumbling of a motorcycle engine, somehow projected from elsewhere.

Adam's eyes open and his head begins to droop forward. Before he can take view of the girl once more, a hand grabs him by the neck and two fingers are pushed painfully up under his chin. Unable to look down any further, he struggles to say, "What the fuck, lady?"

Her mouth begins to work faster, double-time. Somehow, her tongue and lips seem to grow warmer and wetter. A finger—from where, he's not sure—finds his asshole and presses on it gently. Like a button.

Adam bites his tongue and shuts the fuck up.

Julie has taken them far from the camp, much further than she ever would have in her right mind. But things aren't normal right now, far from it. The woods are bursting with magical colors and plants and tiny fairies buzzing through the air like hummingbirds.

Though he's tripped and fallen numerous times, Tommy is still happily giving chase. The eyes above have followed them everywhere, but he doesn't mind. Whenever he looks to the sky, they tell him to hurry, she's getting too far ahead. So, he runs faster and calls after her, laughing.

Ahead of him, Julie slows, hearing voices. She looks back over her shoulder at Tommy, wondering if it's him. But these voices are elsewhere; in the opposite direction of Tommy and speaking in whispers. She scans the trees for their source and spots several large figures in the distance. She moves toward them slowly. At least, she thinks she's moving slowly. Somehow, Tommy seems to be getting farther and farther behind, almost so far that she can't see him anymore when she turns back. But there, maybe thirty feet in front of her, the figures have gathered into a tight circle to converse in hushed tones. There's no mistaking their existence any longer.

She wonders: *What's their secret? Their conspiracy? Their game?*

She becomes giddy with excitement. *Maybe a party is being planned!*

But where the hell is Tommy? She looks over shoulder again in search of him, but her lover has vanished. Maybe he took a wrong turn somewhere along the way? The whispers steal her attention once more, rising as if to draw her back to where she belongs. She nears their gathering and realizes these shapes are actually trees, hunched over as if to crowd something fallen.

"What is it?" she asks upon arrival. "Is something hurt?"

The trees respond to her voice. They twist in place and tower over her, alive.

Though they don't have eyes or ears, they do have mouths. Large mouths full of razor-like teeth dripping with saliva.

Tommy can hear her screaming from somewhere to his right, calling his name. Calling for help. He changes direction and runs at full speed. Around him, things darken in response. The trees become jagged and hunched over. The bushes fill with spiked vines. The eyes overhead grow red and angry. Finally, he sees Julie ahead of him, struggling with five enormous figures hidden in shadow.

"Let her go!" he screams, waving his hands before him. "LET HER GO!"

The figures turn to view him. He can see now that they're actually trees, tall and thick with strong branch-arms ending in clawed hands. Their mouths are hanging open, starved and ready to feed. In their sharp talons, Julie is squirming to break free. She's covered in bloody cuts and her shirt is torn around her stomach. "Help!" she wails with tears in her eyes. "Burn them! Cut them! KILL THEM!"

Tommy skids to a halt, unable to comprehend the scene unfolding for him. Before he can make another move, the trees lift Julie several feet into the air with each of her limbs held by a different gnarled branch. One of the trees tugs her to the left. Another tree tugs her to the right, fighting for her. The one in the back has a grip on her hair and is pulling her head backward roughly as she screams.

"TOMMY! DO SOMETHING!"

Her neck suddenly splits open like a bag of rice, spewing forth a gush of blood. Tommy is drenched in it, frozen in place and sputtering. Julie's eyes are wide as her mouth opens and shuts dumbly, like a fish out of water. A second later, her head is torn free of her body with a sound that brings Velcro shoes to Tommy's mind, the sticking and unsticking of them.

The tree in possession of Julie's head lifts its severed trophy high enough for Tommy to see. Meanwhile, the other monstrosities have continued their tug-of-war, yanking Julie's corpse back and forth. Bones are audibly breaking. Skin is audibly tearing. Blood is freely flowing.

There goes the right leg. Then both arms. Each of the trees has a piece, some larger than others, and now they're feasting on Julie. Her head is being squeezed as the tree holding it arches backward to align its open mouth with her dripping juices. As its grip increases, her eyeballs pop out of their sockets to dangle loosely against the tree's gnarled knuckles. Blood and gore seep out of Julie's ravaged head and into the creature's eager mouth below. Another tree is gnawing on her arm like it's a chicken wing. Somehow, Tommy can still hear her screaming, even though her head has been completely crushed and is now hanging loosely in the monster's hand like a fucking skin mask with broken plates of bone slipping out from the bottom.

Christ, this is a bad trip, Tommy tells himself, blinking through the blood that coats his face. *A* really *fucking bad trip.*

As Julie's midsection is fought over and torn open, organs and lengths of intestine spill onto the leaves at the bases of the trees. Tommy's eyes focus on the shape resembling a water balloon for reasons he cannot explain. He thinks it's Julie's bladder, trembling as if full to burst. Never mind the uncoiled intestines or gallons of blood that are deepening the leaves with sticky crimson. It's the bladder, though, that has Tommy transfixed in horror. It's the bladder that seems to make the whole fucked-up scene real to him.

He blinks and forces his gaze higher. The tree nearest to him has Julie's right leg sticking out of its mouth as it sucks blood from the severed limb like a Popsicle. It turns to face Tommy next—smiling without letting the leg drop—and reaches for him with a bloody claw, greedy for more.

His trance is finally broken. Tommy squeals, turns tail, and runs like hell.

CHAPTER 3

WE INTERRUPT YOUR SEXY TIME WITH THIS IMPORTANT ANNOUNCEMENT

His hands are gentle against her skin. His fingers and palms are coarse—a working man's hands are usually rough—but she likes the way Justin's calluses feel against her thighs. It tickles just a bit, sending goosebumps up her side and spine. They've been kissing for minutes, maybe hours for all she knows, and all is right inside the tent. The screams from the woods cannot be heard. There are only crickets and the crackling fire outside. And their moans, of course. Both Justin and Mary are getting louder, panting like dogs, hungry for one another.

"Do it," she tells him, not needing to specify.

Justin begins to tear off her clothing and his own as they continue to kiss, somehow always keeping their lips pressed. How? *Must be magic*, she tells herself, feeling the sparks of the mushrooms inside her. This is ordained. The spirit guides have ushered away the remaining world so that she can have her man with absolute privacy, free to fuck and lick and suck however long she pleases.

He's inside her now. She doesn't know when it happened or how (shouldn't there have been pain or bleeding?) but he's there, deep inside her and swollen. *The euphoria is helping me*, she thinks. *I don't feel anything bad. Only good.* She smiles and gasps as he begins sliding out, then in. Out. Then in. Harder. Faster. His calloused hands are exploring every inch of her body, as are his tongue and lips. She feels him bite her neck, suck her earlobe, nibble at her breast. When his teeth go as far as to pull her nipple into his mouth, she feels an overflow of wetness between her legs. *Is it his or mine?* She doesn't know, doesn't care. But she has him and they aren't stopping. Not yet. Far from it.

Justin flips her over, lifts up her ass, and buries his mouth between her cheeks. Mary bites the blankets pushed against her face and moans loudly. She's never had this before, either. Everything is new and exciting and surprising. His tongue tickles in a very good way. Then there's his fingers; he's petting her as he feasts, keeping her eager for his cock. Once he's driven himself back inside her, she cums again and squeals from the pleasure. Everything is amazing in the world. Everything is perfect, just the way it should be.

Until it's not.

Tommy is suddenly outside the tent screaming.

"She's dead! She's dead! SHE'S FUCKING DEAD!"

Justin unzips the tent and steps outside, still naked, and breathless. There, he finds his brother pounding the dirt with his fists, covered in blood, and howling as tears run down his cheeks, making paths through the sticky crimson.

"What? Where's Julie?" Justin asks, completely flabbergasted by the scene unfolding before him.

Mary remains in the tent with a blanket wrapped around her sweaty form, unwilling to do what Justin has so boldly done: put himself on display for Tommy.

But Tommy doesn't give a shit about her. He doesn't even see Mary. The only person he sees is his older brother and the cock hanging eye-level with him. He slaps it away from his face and grabs two of the stones securing the pit of fire. In his distress, he throws them into the woods and screams until his voice cracks.

Meanwhile, Justin turns back to Mary and requests his clothes. He's in the process of yanking on his pants when his brother turns hard in the dirt and gets right up in his face, leaving mere inches between them. "Julie's dead," he says with a whimper. "They fucking *ate* her!" Then he's spinning away again and falling to the ground as his body convulses with cries.

Mary doesn't know what to say or do. Justin appears to be just as shocked and confused as she, unwilling to lift his pants any higher than his thighs. They're forgotten, much like she is now.

Overhead, the sky is doing something unnatural. No one seems to notice but Mary. She pokes her head out from the tent and twists her neck awkwardly for a look. The stars have quadrupled in size and are only growing bigger. It's as if a trillion comets are shooting toward the campsite to make ash of them all. Her heart begins to pound inside her chest and she's suddenly unable to catch her breath. She tears her eyes away from the sky, hoping to get Justin's attention, but he's moved away from her. Tommy has launched himself back into the woods with his brother following close behind, blindly tossing over his shirt. No one has said a word to her, asked her to come. They've simply left her to disappear into the swallowing dark, all the while yelling back and forth to one another.

Alone and terrified, Mary pulls her head back inside the tent and secures the entrance zipper. If she can't see the sky, maybe it can't hurt her. Maybe the stars will shrink back to little sparkling pricks. Maybe Justin will come back to sooth her, to hold her close and take her back to bed. That's what she wants more than anything. But now her trip has turned dark once more, and she must find some sort of peace to calm her hallucinations.

"It's all in your head. It's all in your head. Think...think happy thoughts. Think...sexy thoughts. Think Justin. Think Justin's hands. Think Justin's chest."

The blanket droops as she releases a hand to reach between her legs.

"Think Justin's lips. Think Justin's touch. His cock. Hard and..."

Her fingers strum and rub as she continues to direct herself into a happier space of mind. She closes her eyes and focuses on the task at hand. Her body vibrates with pleasure. She no longer hears anything in or outside the tent. The tent may as well be gone. Mary is in the night sky with the stars—the appropriately sized stars, beautiful and warm to gaze upon—curled up alongside them as her body shudders with a revived orgasm.

Then she opens her eyes.

Looks down at the stickiness coating her fingertips. It's red like blood.

And she sees something more.

Something between her legs, sliding out of her swollen vagina. A snake. No, something like a snake but different. Its head is wrong. It has a nose and ears and pale skin. It twists and cranes its neck to face her, and it looks just like...

"Ju-Justin?!"

Mary screams and scoots backward across the tent floor, but the snake is still unraveling out of her vagina. It is still *attached to her*.

"Fuck! Fuck! Fuck!"

She is pressed up against the corner of the tent when the tail finally slips out of her and the snake coils upon itself to look in her direction. Its Justin-face is even more unnerving than the horrifying hybrid Beetlejuice takes on at the stairwell. Unlike *his* head, this creature's face is being pulled back like Silly Putty over someone's knee, thus stretching out Justin's mouth and eyes as he grins at Mary and hisses, "Baaaabbbyyyyyyyy."

She screams again and kicks at the snake with her bare foot. It snaps at her in the same instant and leaves behind two puncture marks near her ankle. Mary scurries across the perimeter of the tent floor, barely dodging the snake's additional strikes, and launches herself outside into the dirt. She quickly spins in place, finds the zipper, and seals the tent. Inside, the snake whips around angrily, hissing her name.

Mary lays back onto her elbows and breathes heavily. Her ankle is stinging and swollen from where she was bit. Bursts of colors dance before her eyes, and she does her best to shake them away.

Great, she thinks. *Something else to make me hallucinate.*

But she couldn't have imagined that snake—it bit her, injured her. It must be real then. Somehow.

Tears fill her eyes as she lowers her face and screams. Her hands run through her hair and grab it in fistfuls.

It is then that she realizes she is naked and alone with blood staining her inner thighs. Everyone has fled into the forest, leaving her to fend for herself. And she doesn't know the first thing about surviving in the wild.

Now what do I do? she asks herself.

From inside the tent, the snake continues to taunt her.

"Maaaarrrrrryyyyyyyyy…"

"Tommy! Slow down!"

Justin pauses to catch his breath. His brother is ahead of him, wildly weaving in and out of the trees in search of Julie. Does he have any clue as to where they're going? Justin looks back over his shoulder and realizes the glow of the campfire is no longer visible. All he can see is darkness in every direction. It seems deeper than it should be, as if his eyes are unable to adjust. He's already run into several trees and bruised himself along his arms and legs. His face is covered in scratches and his lip feels wet with blood.

"Tommy! Wait up!"

His brother is far enough ahead now that Justin can barely see his movement. He tries to catch up but trips on something and falls hard. It feels like vines are grabbing hold of his ankles, but he can't see them for himself. The darkness is continuing to deepen around him, swallowing Justin whole. He screams for his brother but there's no response.

Where has Tommy gone? Does he not realize Justin is no longer with him?

Fuck.

Justin stands, dusts himself off, and looks toward the sky for navigation.

The stars are gone.

"It gets better…"

Something skitters through the leaves to his left. He's still in mid-turn when something else shuffles up a tree behind him. Spooked, Justin holds his breath and counts to ten. He hears nothing during that time and relaxes. He takes a step forward—in the general direction he *thinks* Tommy was headed—and stops immediately when something falls loudly from the sky, landing before him. It's massive in girth and height. Justin cranes his head upward to identify his visitor and realizes that it is some sort of troll. It must be eight feet tall and as thick around as an architectural column. Its skin is a forest green and covered in boils and small tufts of hair. Its nose is bulbous, its cheeks are plump, and its mouth shelters rows of tiny, sharp teeth. The eyes are the worst, though; they are a sickly yellow with red swirls that continue to move in a hypnotic spiral.

"What are…"

Before he can finish, the monster grabs him with a massive hand, yanks him close, and then launches him backward twenty feet. Justin smacks into a tree hard enough that he's left gasping for air with an invading darkness swarming his vision. He rolls over and groans, blinking and looking for his assailant. Though the pain is shocking, the fact that he can move is a good sign.

The troll—or whatever it was—has vanished.

Justin stands slowly and leans against the tree that

stopped him soaring through the air. He searches the darkness for movement or unfamiliar shapes but sees nothing of concern. He must have imagined the encounter. He tries calling for Tommy again but is met with silence. He stretches painfully and begins to walk. It isn't long before the leaves overhead shake with something heavy.

Shit.

Of course, it returned to the trees. Where else would it have gone? You can't simply hide something that big on the forest floor.

Justin hesitates to look up and is frightened to see numerous pairs of eyes, all of which are yellow with moving spirals of red. Then there are voices echoing inside his head, dozens of them that speak at once: *Seek the clearings. Seek the halos. Step inside and feed the sky.*

"What the hell does that mean?"

The spirals move faster, becoming more hypnotic. Justin feels a paralysis overtake him. The voices continue. More eyes appear. They are everywhere, but how? Shouldn't the trees break under their weight? Tip downward and snap? Groan and scream? The troll he saw was enormous. Is it hugging the body of the tree? Is it something capable of shapeshifting, perhaps? What other explanation is there?

I'm still hallucinating, he tells himself. *It's just the shrooms. I'm probably not even in the woods right now.*

What about Mary? Did he really go into the tent with her? Kiss her? Touch her? Fuck her?

The voices bring him back to the woods, louder and more insistent than before:

Feed the sky! Feed the sky! Feed the sky!

Something new comes over Justin, replacing his paralysis.

It's obedience.

He agrees to find the clearing, and leaves the sea of sickly eyes behind in favor of moving deeper into the mountain, where things can and will only get worse.

The orgasm causes Adam to shudder and moan. When he opens his eyes again, the hand around his throat drops and he's able to view his redheaded pleasurer once more. She has a satisfied look on her face as she tips her head back from him.

"That was fantastic," he tells her, taking a deep breath and releasing it slowly. "Goddamn."

The redhead smiles widely, allowing an overflow of semen to roll down her chin. Disgusted, Adam takes a step back and begins to collect his pants from around his ankles. As he tries to fit his hardened cock back into his underwear, the girl uses her tongue to collect whatever has dribbled down over her chin and says, "We must not waste." She swallows his load and smacks her lips several times, as if to detect a specific ingredient in his batter. A moment later, her eyes flash with excitement and she stands. "Finally. An adequate candidate."

"Huh? A candidate for what?"

Her eyes meet his once more and her demeanor changes. "You are the vessel we've been searching for. One that can bring Him home. And just in time for the prophecy to turn in our favor." She is no longer there to pleasure him; a severe seriousness has befallen her.

Adam laughs uncomfortably and says, "You have a wild imagination, you know that?"

Someone with powerful hands takes hold of him from

behind and squeezes his biceps in warning. He tries to look back to see who's there, but the redhead takes hold of his chin, forcing it forward. She brings his face within an inch of her own and absently licks her sticky lips. "You're coming with us, Adam."

"Did I...tell you my name?"

The redhead grins in a knowing way. "It wasn't necessary to do so."

As she turns from him, the person behind Adam shoves him forward to follow.

Tommy is moving downhill, too quickly to control himself. He tumbles and rolls, slamming against the trees and flinging over bushes on his way to the bottom. When he meets it—hard—he groans and cries out. He feels worse than a broken man; he feels downright crazy, out of his fucking mind.

What did he see back there? Did Julie *really* get torn to pieces and eaten by trees with razor-like teeth?

"No," he tells himself as firmly as he can manage. "No, you imagined that." He stands and takes a cursory look around. The sky overhead is still watching him, but no longer in amusement. The eyes seem to be tracking him instead, studying his every action along the way.

"Fuck off," he tells them, wiping tears from his cheeks. "Fucking mushrooms were tainted." He thrusts an accusatory finger at the sky. "You're not real. You're just...a waking nightmare. You can't do shit to me."

As if to meet his challenge, the forest floor begins to shake and crumble. Tommy jumps back, but it's not enough. The ground releases beneath his feet and he falls into an underground tunnel lit by mounted torches. As he collects himself from the dirt, he eyes the forest overhead, trying to judge the distance he's just dropped. It's high enough that he can't simply climb his way back outside.

"Damn it. Now what?"

A groan echoes from nearby. He turns from the ledge above to look down the tunnel instead. Ahead of him, the ceiling is still intact, suffocating and claustrophobic. Tommy inches forward, not sure where else he can go. He turns to look behind him, but there's no difference. Either way, he has a torch-lit path to follow into the unknown.

He swallows hard and adjusts his pants.

Here goes nothing.

Mary is shaking outside of the tent with her arms wrapped around herself. The pack with all her clothing is still inside, out of reach. She collects herself from the dirt and moves toward the fire, not only for its warmth, but its presumed protection. Inside the tent, the snake with Justin's face continues to whip around frantically, as if in a struggle with some unknown force. She considers fleeing into the darkened woods to find the others but knows she shouldn't leave the camp.

It would be suicidal, she tells herself. *I'll get lost and starve. I don't even have my shoes!*

And what about weapons? Did they have anything here she could use in a fight? Mary turns to the various packs littering the clearing and begins to frantically search them as the tent continues to bat around from the inside.

"Sssssssss...Maaarrrrrryyyyyyyyy..."

She does her best to ignore the snake's call and turns

over another pack, shaking it violently as if throttling a longtime bully. She finds a large hunting knife amidst a collection of cooking utensils and nearly cheers aloud. She tears off its sheath and turns to face the tent, ready for anything. The snake seems to sense this and stills. She waits for one beat, then another. The tent is quiet and motionless.

Did it die?

No, of course not, you idiot. It's a trap.

She imagines the fish guy from *Star Wars* and giggles.

She's still high. This could all be in her head, something she'll laugh about in the morning once she's come down from the shrooms. How many did she eat? Adam was comforting her by the fire, feeding her gently as if the psychedelics were chocolate-covered strawberries. Maybe she had more than she realized. That could explain how strange things had become in the last hour.

Silence descends on the camp, making Mary turn in place. Suddenly, the zippered entrance of the tent bursts open by force and Justin's stretched face soars through the air.

"MARY!"

The snake whips itself around her neck and immediately constricts. As it squeezes shut her throat, cutting off her ability to breathe, it repeatedly hisses her name.

Mary gasps and claws at her neck to no avail while the sky overhead continues to burn with meteor showers that only she can see. A farewell celebration, perhaps.

CHAPTER 4

IMPOSSIBLE THINGS AND SWALLOWING DARKNESS

Justin has been wandering for what feels like hours. He is hungry and thirsty and exhausted. He's just about forgotten what he's looking for—his hypnotic obedience fading with distance from the trolls—when a clearing ahead of him catches his eye. In its center, there appears to be someone floating in the air, gently rotating in place, still and quiet. Justin approaches the spot slowly, all the while searching the surrounding forest for something that could be watching him from hiding.

"Hey, pal? You okay?" Justin asks, inching closer to the backside of the form.

Whoever it is doesn't reply. Justin eyes them from top to bottom. They're wearing a dark shirt and shorts with boots and an empty holster strapped to their calf. They're at least two feet above the ground, maybe three. Atop the leaves, not far from the circle, is a revolver. Upon seeing it, Justin pauses once more to consider the scene. He waits and listens, for what he is not sure.

"Buddy?"

Nothing.

The body is slowly rotating in place as Justin watches. It is nearly facing him now, enough so that he can see it's a man in the halo of moonlight with his mouth hanging open and his head tilted back. It looks as if he died viewing the sky.

Yes, *died*. This is clearly a corpse. There's a hole in the man's temple, though very little blood. Perhaps this was the entry wound then. There's practically nothing on the man himself, just some faint staining down the front of his shirt. But there is something odd about the skin of his face currently visible to Justin. It looks raw and stripped, perhaps burned.

The body continues to rotate to face him.

Justin finally finds his nerve to step to the side so that he can view the corpse head-on. The man's face is pink with slashes of exposed muscle. He appears to have been entertained by the sky, because he is staring upward. However, his eyes are missing. All that remains are small globs of mushy white in each socket. His jaw is slack, and his tongue is hanging limply from the corner of his mouth. It appears shriveled, badly enough so that it could crumble if touched. In fact, the entire man appears shriveled and drained, as if he were near starvation prior to his floating predicament. Is this why he used the gun on himself? Oddly enough, the exit wound isn't bloody either, despite its size.

It takes Justin a moment to piece it all together, but he eventually realizes the poor bastard is drying like jerky right before his eyes. Tiny pieces of skin are flaking off him and floating overhead, into the night sky. It's as if the man is being depleted right here in this circular space. His arms and shins are stripped much like his face, exposing the pink of muscle and the white of bone. Justin wonders how the man has fared under his clothes but does not dare check. Perhaps it is only what's visible that it is being pulled off. Then again, the man's frame looks brittle and thin, suggesting all of him is being reduced to a husk.

Feed the sky.

He hears the voices in his head once more and shudders. This is what they wanted of him. To step into a halo and be stuck forever.

Justin turns and searches the area. This spot isn't the only one in the clearing. Several other halos are visible along the forest floor.

He returns his gaze to the levitating corpse. The sight chills him to his core.

"Jesus..."

He suddenly feels very exposed in the clearing. He considers the way he came, knowing it is safe (or *was*, for a time), but thinking he should continue looking for his brother. Upon collecting the fallen revolver from beside the dead man, he crosses the clearing, all the while avoiding the other halos at all costs. Just to keep smart, as opposed to careless. He'll live longer that way.

Adam is being directed through the woods by several women. There's the naked girl and two others in crimson cloaks. The redhead is acting like their leader. Behind Adam is someone else, though he has no idea as to who. Several times, they've pushed him to keep pace, though. He suspects the person is frightfully large because their hands have covered the width of his back with every shove.

"Not much further," the redhead says, looking briefly over her shoulder at him and smiling. Adam has not been able to go a minute without watching the sway of her bare ass ahead of them, and she clearly knows it. But does she know her scars are leaving him chilled to the bone? She is crisscrossed with marks, some white and healed, others red and scabbed. They nearly cover her entire body, from her neck down to her ankles. There must be hundreds of them, but why?

The other two women keep their eyes forward and say nothing as they escort him. Adam has only seen glimpses of their faces so far. They appeared out of nowhere when he was first taken, as if they were given a signal to join the party. Adam can only hope they're as pretty as their leader; if this is some sort of cult orgy deal, he wants it to be picture-perfect. However, the kidnapper with the large hands behind him is troubling. Hopefully, they're just some sort of enforcer. Or maybe a cameraman.

After several minutes have passed, they come to a thick tree that is laden with carved symbols Adam has never seen. Even stranger is their pulsing glow. The pleasurer taps the tree rhythmically, says something Adam does not understand, and then traces her finger from the base of the tree to the height of her head.

"We've arrived," she says, stepping to the side. Adam is shoved forward, closer to the tree. Its bark peels back to reveal a bright and blinding doorway standing slightly taller than him, its edges red as if burning.

"Arrived where?" he asks, blinking back the stars that now crowd his vision.

In lieu of an answer, someone shoves him forward. This time, something from the light grabs ahold of him and yanks him away from the others.

He begins to fall as if from a great height.

Mary is close enough to the fire that her skin is burning. Despite the pain, she is too busy to give it any attention. The snake with Justin's face is wrapped around her neck, constricting tighter and tighter. Her knife has fallen in their struggle, and she can't see it from her current position in the dirt, kicking and gasping for air. She desperately claws at the snake, trying for just an inch so that she can breathe again. The snake's head turns to face her directly, bringing her eye to eye with Justin.

"Maaaarrrrryyyyyyyyyyssssssssssssssssssssssssss…"

She wants to scream at the bastard but gags instead. Finally, she throws herself into the fire and rolls. The temporary assault of heat is just enough to make the snake relax its grip. Mary pulls hard and is rewarded with a second of blissful oxygen. But just as quickly as it came, it is gone. The snake constricts once more. The difference this time is Mary has spotted her fallen knife nearby, thanks to that brief moment of clarity. She kicks the dirt repeatedly to inch herself toward it. Finally, she can feel the hilt against her fingertips. One more kick ought to do it…

"Maaaarrrryyyyyyyyyyssssss?"

She takes hold of the knife and swiftly plunges it into the snake, so deep that she can feel the pressure of the blade against her neck. The creature screams and unravels from her, dropping unceremoniously to the dirt and squirming by the fire as blood spurts from the base of the knife. Mary tries to stand but immediately falls, too weak and still coughing. Luckily, she is no longer being attacked. She takes a moment against one of the logs and collects herself as the snake whips around the campsite in pain. The Justin-face is howling and transforming, into what she cannot tell. It contorts and bloats and shrinks and splits, again and again.

Finally, Mary has had enough. She grabs the flailing snake by its whipping tail and tosses it into the fire. The creature writhes and screams from within the flames, but not for long. It quickly begins to expand as if filling with radioactivity, and explodes into a hundred small pieces of gore, painting the campsite with blood. Mary drops into a nearby chair and gently touches her bruised neck. She leans back, takes a deep breath, and shuts her eyes.

She wonders where the others have gone and when they'll be coming back. Her ankle throbs as it continues to swell and change color.

Tommy has been following the tunnel for some time. It's cold and poorly lit. Every so often, he hears a groan or scream that sets him on edge. He's yet to find a way out and worries the tunnel will stretch so far that he'll simply starve to death before ever reaching its end.

"Hello? Anyone out there?"

There is no answer to his tepid call. But ahead in the darkness, he sees a crumpled form on the ground. He slows as he approaches it, unsure of what he's found. Once he's within five feet of it, he realizes the form belongs to a naked person curled into the fetal position, covered in mud and blood. They're backside is facing him.

"Jesus. Are you okay?" he asks, taking a knee at their feet.

They don't move for him, nor do they speak. Tommy swallows back his fear as best he can and reaches out to grip the person's shoulder. When he turns them over onto their back, he sees a woman's brutalized body. As she's rolled toward Tommy, her breasts slip to each armpit, loose from breastfeeding. There's a cesarean scar, still healing, above her pelvis, red and sticky with blood. Bruises cover her body haphazardly from a beating. Her left ankle is nearly detached from the cut of a blade, possibly to trip her.

Worst of all, the woman's head is missing.

Tommy stumbles backward, sick to his stomach. Whatever was used to remove the dead mother's head was jagged; the skin along her severed neck hangs in strips of various lengths.

There's no helping this poor soul. Tommy pulls his eyes away from her and continues through the tunnel, shaken to his core. Farther ahead, he spots another corpse, this one older and rotten. Instead of taking a closer look, he hurries around it.

Several minutes later, the path begins to curve. It's the first deviation he's seen.

"Finally, a welcomed change..."

Something scurries beyond the curve, casting a shadow along the wall that dances in the flickering torch glow, exaggerated and unrecognizable. Tommy pauses, not sure what he's just seen or what awaits him. Possibly a rat he scared off from its meal. With two corpses nearby, the rodent would have plenty to eat upon its return.

He considers calling out again in case it's a person. When he opens his mouth to do so, he thinks better of it and clenches his teeth instead. He hesitates to move or even breathe, in fear of giving away his location. Whatever or whoever is ahead of him could be very dangerous. They could have been responsible for the bodies. After what he's seen tonight—or at least *thinks* he's seen—Tommy should assume everything is dangerous.

He wonders if the eyes in the sky are still somehow watching him, even though he is underground now.

Despite the shifting shadow dropping into the dark floor and vanishing, he can still hear distant movement around the bend. Should he continue forward? What else is there to do? Turn back and wander for who-knows-how-many-miles in the opposite direction, beyond the collapsed earth that birthed him?

"Fuck it."

He moves forward, but only a few inches at a time. He's terrified and without protection. Eventually, he reaches the sharp turn and sticks his head out without exposing too much of his body in the process. Though he does not see any animal or being, he can make out new shapes along the floor, against the tunnel walls. He brings his whole body around the tunnel's curve and inches forward. As he nears the first shape, the more he's confused by what he sees.

"Is that...Are those...?"

He's within several feet of it now. He positions himself before the nearest shape and takes a knee.

"Jesus Christ."

It's a head. Well, part of a head. What would normally exist above the bridge of the nose has been severed and discarded elsewhere. What remains are the nostrils, cheeks, and mouth. The half-head rests upon a shredded neck that has been impaled upon a spike lifting up from the floor. Resting atop its pierced tongue is a candle with a flame that flickers through the half-head's hollowed nostrils. The display is reminiscent of a Jack-O-Lantern, perhaps the kind devils might carve in hell.

There are more of them, of course. Every thirty feet or

so is another half-head, their lights meager but upsetting, nevertheless. Tommy stands and turns away from the lantern at his feet. He does not wish to look at these horrible things any longer. He does his best to keep his eyes off the floor where the horrible decorations line the walls but it's difficult to pretend they're not there.

He's only gone a hundred yards when something impossible happens. Something that makes him piss his pants on the spot.

The half-heads all begin to impossibly scream in unison.

Surely, he's lost. The sky has darkened like ink, making it impossible for Justin to see anything. There is no moon, no stars, no glow of anything to light his way. Even the surrounding trees seem to have darkened, as if scorched by fire. Maybe that's what has happened here.

Justin moves slowly through the black, his hands held out before him as he stumbles over branches and brush. Occasionally, he bumps against a tree or feels something snagging his ankles. He tries not to think about it too much. He feels crazy enough as it is without the consideration of a living, breathing forest interested in killing him.

There are two tents ahead of him, maybe large enough to each cover two or three people. He rushes toward them, hoping the campers are inside, but finds each one empty. The fire pit between them is cold and damp from the overnight dew; it doesn't appear to have been lit recently. Inside the tents, there are multiple open packs of clothing and supplies. He searches through them for anything of use, such as a compass or a cellphone with a signal but comes up with nothing better than a lantern. It looks as if someone has already sorted through the things before him, maybe someone that didn't belong there either.

Justin switches on the lantern, checks around the outside of the campsite for anything else, and curses. It doesn't look like the owners ever finished unloading their bags after setting up the tents, seeing how little there is to be found. Perhaps they left in a hurry. Only for a moment does he wonder why. Then it seems obvious. Maybe the man in the moonlit halo was one of the campers staying here. Justin wonders what must have happened to the others. Had they been separated prior to his demise?

He curses again and turns to leave the abandoned tents. With the lantern outstretched before him, he carves deeper into the forest and calls out his brother's name. Before long, he's lost and wondering how long he's been gone from Mary. Minutes seem to pass like hours. He is not at all sure how long ago he stumbled upon the tents. Already, he can barely remember them.

An orb of white appears several hundred yards ahead as he considers stopping to rest. Though it is shrouded by the surrounding trees, the object's glow is intense enough that it cannot be missed in the surrounding darkness. Justin adjusts his course and directs himself toward it. Once he is nearly upon the orb, he grows cautious once more. It's levitating in place (much like the camper's corpse in the halo) and is as large as a basketball. This close, it is nearly blinding.

Justin circles the light, curiously drawn to the object like a moth to flame—it's all he can see and all he wants to see. He is mesmerized.

Wait.

Something's not right, he's suddenly sure of it. It's as if he struggling to wake from a daze.

This seems familiar, he thinks. *Isn't there a fish that hunts its prey this way? With a lure...*

The ground shudders beneath his feet. Tall, tightly clustered spikes shoot upward from the leaves, cutting off his escape. He drops the stolen lantern by his feet and grabs hold of the spikes like prison bars. As he tries forcing his face between them, he screams uselessly for help. The orb behind him begins to vibrate, drawing him to look over his shoulder. A bioluminescent light extends down from the orb and into the earth. Then it spreads in every direction, illuminating the outline of its stalk and the mouth he is standing inside. Overheard, as high as the trees, it seems, Justin can see the top row of toothpick teeth waiting to clench. If he's not gone before this monster's mouth closes, he's fucked.

Justin eyes the orb once more. Is it a tongue of some sort or maybe a uvula? Does it really matter? He quickly launches himself onto the stalk and holds on for dear life. The mouth shudders again, this time rising from the soil as the creature abandons its hiding place in the ground. Justin cannot see its shape beyond the teeth, but it must be rather large to hold him with its mouth open and plenty of room to spare. As he clings onto the orb's stalk, he is lifted higher and higher into the air. Soon, they are just above the treetops, nearly one with the inky sky.

The darkness changes.

The black blinks with a million eyes that turn on him, furious and hungry. Justin swivels his neck, trying to spot them all, but he can only see so much with the roof of the creature's mouth blocking whatever is overhead. He decides to look for the throat and turns. Thanks to the glowing eyes, he can see its descent. The downward slope is located mere feet from the orb, smaller than he would have expected. His lantern soon rolls down into the cavern and vanishes.

The jaw closes around Justin then, and the sky-spread eyes disappear. Worst of all, the orb seems to power down, its glow fading to black. Once again, he's being swallowed by a suffocating darkness.

Justin fingers the recovered gun in his back pocket and starts to consider his options.

CHAPTER 5

THE WHITE RITUAL, AS PERFORMED BY THE CRIMSON HIGHNESS

When Adam stops falling, it's as if he's woken from a dream. He opens his eyes and finds himself lying atop a blanket woven with symbols he's never seen. Symbols like the ones found on the tree that dropped him there.

Adam props himself up on his elbows and looks around. There are large fires to his left and right, lighting the enormous clearing. Standing around those fires and his blanket are more women in crimson cloaks. His original pleasurer sits cross-legged at his feet, still naked but covered in red body paint that hides her many scars.

"What happened to you?" he asks her.

"I've prepared."

"For...?"

"For the ceremony."

There's a sinking feeling in the pit of Adam's stomach.

He eyes the many robed women again. "What are they all here for?"

"For you."

"Gee, I'm energetic but I don't know if I can manage all these women in one night."

"You won't be."

He looks at the mysterious leader again. "What do you mean? Where are we? What are we doing here?"

"You are an acceptable vessel for our prophecy to be fulfilled. I've *tasted* it."

"Do you...want me to impregnate someone?"

"No. Our Lord will come from you."

Adam chews on those words before replying, "I'm getting mixed signals here."

The fires on either side of him turn white and translucent, like ghostly portals to the dead.

"What the hell?"

The redheaded leader nods to a robed woman nearby, then stands. The follower takes her place at Adam's ankles and bears down on them to keep him from kicking. Before he can react, two more robed women appear beside him to shove down his shoulders. Another two approach to secure his wrists. They have him pinned in a second.

"What is this?" he demands, flexing against their surprising strength. "Who the hell are you people?"

The painted woman stands herself over him and bends her knees to take a seat atop his chest, her legs spreading to reveal the little tuft of red between her thighs. "I am the Crimson Highness," she tells him as her nails dig slightly into his chest. "And this is the White Ritual."

Adam studies her for a moment—*all* of her—before smiling. "Well, you didn't have to hold me down to climb on top, but I've been restrained before and I must admit, I like it."

The girl smiles and licks her lips. She then leans forward and kisses him hungrily. Adam's cock swells immediately behind her. For a moment, all is well again. Adam loves the way the leader flicks her tongue in his mouth, probing his gums and teeth as if in search of hidden treasure. He's about to fight against his restraints for control when something changes.

There's more than just an unfamiliar tongue inside his mouth now.

He tries struggling but cannot move himself away. He shakes his head back and forth, but the pleasurer grabs his skull tightly in her grip and keeps him still. Whatever has crawled up and out of her throat is now slithering across his tongue. He tries to cough—a pre-choke, if you will—to push back the creature, but the little bastard is persistent and surprisingly strong. It forces itself into his throat and worms its way down into his belly.

Finally, the leader pulls back her mouth and smiles with bloodied teeth. Adam curses and spits at her, demanding an explanation. "What the unholy fuck was that?"

The leader wipes the blood from her lips and stands. "Our Lord's seed."

Adam gags uselessly. "That's disgusting, lady. Just admit you slipped a slug into my mouth and call out the cameraman. Good show, you had your fucking laughs. Now let me up!"

His stomach suddenly rumbles and twists painfully. He yelps in surprise and fights against his restraints once more. When nobody loosens their grip, he searches the faces of the robed women that surround him. He tries reading their expressions but all he sees is excitement and wonder. He's starting to think this is more of a sacrifice than a prank.

"Please. It hurts," he pleads. "Let me go."

The spectators lean forward for a closer look as Adam's stomach visibly moves beneath his shirt. The pain is so intense that he shuts his eyes, grinds his teeth, and throws back his head in the dirt. Finally, he erupts in a hellish howl.

"FUCKKKKKK!"

Someone smacks him across the face with something heavy, perhaps a branch, and Adam bites through his tongue. He curses but his speech is now slurred and mostly unintelligible. Blood begins to fill his mouth, which causes him to sputter. There's another hit, this time harder, and he is knocked unconscious.

With their vessel still, the robed women begin to strip Adam of his clothes. As they yank down his pants, his naked midsection begins to blush and bruise in deep reds and purples.

"He's coming," the Crimson Highness announces to her sisters from between the whitened fires. As if on cue, their flames begin to spin wildly into thick vortexes that stretch upward into the night sky and turn the clouds red. The eyes that replaced the stars have grown wide and joyful.

Mary is inside the tent getting dressed when she hears movement along the cliffside beyond their campsite. She stiffens and listens carefully for more. Someone is creeping along the vicinity of the tent, maybe ten feet away from her. She can hear every footstep they take. They sound light on their feet but after what she's seen tonight, Mary wants to prepare for the worst. The problem is her knife is in the fire and there's nothing to defend herself with from inside the tent. She quickly laces her boots—careful not to worsen her injured ankle—and begins outside to face her new tormentor, not at all ready for a physical encounter.

The sky immediately catches her off-guard. The meteors have been replaced. Now there's a sea of blood overheard backdropping a million glowing eyes that are focused elsewhere on the mountain. They appear bright and joyful, despite the spreading crimson. But then they turn on Mary, seeming to sense her gaze. Their joyfulness shifts to disgust, then to...

Fear?

Mary stumbles backward and falls. From her place in the dirt, she stares at the eyes in disbelief as the sky blossoms beyond them, replacing the black of space with blood. She then spots the white vortexes feeding into the sky, pulsing and pumping the red.

Something bad is clearly happening.

Before she can think much else of this development, hands grasp her shoulders from behind and drag her into the cliffside brush.

Tommy is sure he's near the end of the tunnel now that the half-heads are screaming as loudly as humanly possible. This must be their crescendo, the tunnel's big reveal just around the bend.

"Just get me the hell out of here," he mumbles as the walls curve once more. His head is splitting from the screams and his underwear has gotten cold from his piss soaking in it for so long.

Ahead, there is finally a faint glow of light that stretches wider than anything produced by the lanterns.

"Oh, thank God."

After another minute of walking, he can see the exit. Outside, there appears to be a campsite, though it is not his own. What else could cause such a fantastic glow in the middle of the night in the middle of the forest? There must be a fire pit nearby that is enormous.

As he comes to the end of the tunnel, Tommy makes sure to kick over the last half-head he passes, filling its mouth with dirt and distinguishing its flame. "Fucking thing," he spits, making a hundred and eighty degree turn to see where the tunnel has let him out. There's a cliffside stretching far above its mouth, much higher than he would have guessed.

Did I really travel so deeply underground?

Perhaps he moved downhill at a gradual rate, he decides, reminding himself they're atop a mountain.

Behind him, flames roar. He turns to see not one but two pits of fire. They're white in color and twisting into the night sky. He looks up at the blooming red above and shudders. The eyes are out and celebrating. Whatever is happening can't be good. Had they known the fate that awaited Julie when viewing their chase through the woods? How long ago had that been? It feels like hours have passed. Tommy can't be sure it ever happened. He hopes Julie is still back at camp, wondering where the hell he's run off to. Perhaps all of this has been a bad trip. There were no hungry trees or screaming half-heads lining a secret underground tunnel. And this place, with the fires? Another hallucination. He's tired and will soon fall asleep. In the morning, he will find himself in the tent with Julie's shapely ass pressed against his cock. Just as God intended.

This is what he tells himself, as if that will make it true.

He stumbles away from the tunnel and toward the two fires on unsteady legs. Between them, a small crowd has gathered in robed garments. It takes him a moment to count the figures as he nears, but there's at least seven on the outside circle. He thinks there are others in the middle but it's difficult to tell. Off to the side, nearly hidden in shadow, is a large shape that makes him stop in his tracks. Has he been seen? He waits a moment for a reaction, but none comes. He's still in the darkness, ignored.

The large figure isn't human, he doesn't think. It's shaped like a man—even resembles a man—but is far bigger than any man Tommy has ever seen. Its arms are as thick as its waist, and its hands are as wide as shovel heads. Tattoos of dancing flames stretch across its skin, intertwined with small eyes.

Like the fires in this camp, Tommy realizes, the ink is white.

Just what the hell is all this?

The crowd shifts, just enough for him to see a naked woman wearing red body paint. At her feet, someone is lying in the dirt, their clothing tossed aside. The woman says something to her robed accomplices in the ring, and they move back several paces to give the body room. Tommy counts thirteen cultists, not including the large figure in the shadows.

He carefully moves closer—keeping against the trees and brush as he goes—and finally recognizes the man on the ground.

"Adam? What the fuck?"

Though his friend appears to be unconscious or dead, his stomach is moving. There's a bulge in its center, a bulge that is actively pushing outward in different directions.

Blood appears around Adam's mouth as he groans loudly.

So, *not* dead. But probably close to it.

What the fuck do I do?

He's already lost Julie; he can't lose Adam, too. Tommy looks around his feet for anything he can use as a weapon. There's nothing but sticks and some rocks that have tumbled down the cliffside. He collects a stone from beside his shoe, judges its weight, and figures he can at least cause a distraction.

"Better than nothing..."

He looks toward the group again. Adam's midsection appears to be deeply bruised all over. Perhaps, it's about to split. What is happening to him? What is inside his stomach? Is there anything Tommy can do to stop it?

Just then, Adam bursts open. Coils and chunks of intestine are tossed into the air like confetti. Acid and blood and remains of food spray the robed women and their painted leader. Rather than scream and run, they stand their ground and watch Adam intently. Though his eyes have opened, they appear lifeless. Whatever is happening, this cult has just killed Tommy's friend. His grip on the stone tightens and he rears back his hand to throw it when—

Eerrraaaaaaahhhh!

The inhuman cry stops Tommy in his tracks.

From Adam's exploded midsection, a white demon drenched in blood and shit is climbing to its feet. It's perhaps six inches tall and sharp looking in every way, as if it's made of razor blades and barbed wire. Its eyes are black and bulbous, its fingers long and pointed, and its frame slender and toned. When it howls again, Tommy sees its jaw extend several inches, nearly half its height.

The painted woman holds her hands to the sky and

sings praises for the birth of the creature. Her robed friends drop to their knees and bow as they begin chanting something in an unfamiliar language. The large figure off to the side is...

Gone.

"Shit."

An enormous hand grabs Tommy's wrist and yanks it backward. The stone he's been holding drops to the ground as a bone in his wrist snaps through the skin with an audible crack. Tommy screams in pain as he's spun around to face the behemoth. It stands at least a foot taller than him with a chest as broad as a door. Its head is shaped like a torpedo, hairless and slick and coming to a rounded point. Its eyes are completely white and all the more piercing because of it.

Tommy whimpers in the beast's grip and asks, "What *are* you?"

The enormous man—assuming it's even human—doesn't answer him. Instead, it drags Tommy toward the women as they continue their worship of the small demon bathed in Adam's blood. The painted leader is the first to see their visitor, and she responds with a smile.

"Excellent! A snack."

Tommy tries to twist away from the behemoth but can't free his broken wrist. "A snack? What the fuck do you mean by *snack*?" he cries, searching for answers from the robed women on their knees. They all look at him with empty eyes and expressionless faces.

"Our Ground Lord is famished," the leader says, spreading open her arms. "But first, He must be baptized in fire."

The small demon steps out of Adam's exploded midsection and approaches one of the white fires.

Overheard, the night sky has turned completely crimson. The eyes have gathered close together above the camp for a better look. They watch every step the demon takes with wild anticipation. It approaches the fire, howls, and steps into the flames.

Tommy looks away and instead searches his surroundings for a means of escape. If the behemoth is distracted, even for a second, maybe he can make a mad dash for his life. These people are crazy and that...*thing* couldn't have willingly burned itself alive, could it have?

As if to answer his unspoken question, the creature stands from the fire with its broad torso hunched forward. It is at least nine feet taller than before, with skin scorched black and blistered pink with sinewy muscle. Its eyes have yellowed into fascinating orbs and its fingers have extended into curled blades that stretch out at least a foot in length. When the demon straightens its spine fully and stretches out in every direction—its body crackling loudly in response—it towers over them all an additional six feet. It now stands as high as some of the younger trees, nearly three times the height of anyone standing beneath it.

The painted leader bows to the demon and gestures to Tommy. "Your first meal, my Lord."

The demon cocks its head to the side and studies Tommy as he fights the guard's grip in a final, frantic bid for escape. "Please. Please! Let me go!"

The demon grins, revealing a hundred tiny, sharp teeth. It reaches out for Tommy and picks him up by wrapping its incredibly long fingers around his chest. Tommy gasps for air as his ribs crunch beneath its grip. The demon brings him face to face with it and says something in an unfamiliar language.

Tommy continues to beg for his life as tears fill his eyes.

The demon chuckles and uses its free hand to grasp Tommy's ankles firmly. It then yanks down hard on his legs, pulling the young man apart. As Tommy's lower half drops unceremoniously to the dirt, he screams hysterically and feels the blood drain from his heart and head. His eyes roll back, and he takes his last shuddering breath.

The demon then holds Tommy's severed torso over its mouth and begins to feast upon his dangling innards. Once it's sucked out most of its prey's meaty parts, it balls up the flappy remains and lays it onto its long, wicked tongue to roll back into its throat. The demon then retrieves Tommy's lower half from the leaves and begins biting off large pieces while the painted woman speaks to it.

"There are others. Here, on the mountain. Feed on them and continue to grow, my Lord," she says.

With a leg sticking out from its mouth, the demon turns to the cliff side to begin its climb out of the hidden valley.

CHAPTER 6

A STOWAWAY REVEALS HERSELF TO THE "ONE" THAT CAN DEFEAT HIM

The girl crouching beside her appears feral. Her eyes are constantly darting from side to side as her head twitches in response to every sound heard outside their hidey-hole. She's young, probably sixteen or so, likely in high school still. But her clothes are tattered and dirty, as is her skin. It looks as if someone dropped her off in the middle of the forest to learn survival the hard way. Maybe she's the better half of a modern-day Hansel and Gretel fairytale.

It seems that Mary has been holding her breath for several minutes now. She isn't sure why this girl threw them into a spacious hole in the ground, but she thinks it must be for their protection. If only the poor thing would say something! Explain! Instead, she looks around wildly, ears to the exit, vigilant. Breathless.

But Mary can't match her any longer and gasps for air.

The girl glares at her, but only for a moment. Then she returns her gaze to the sky above their cavern, where the void is red and littered with searching eyes.

Searching for them?

It certainly feels like they're hiding. Why else hold up underground? Do the eyes want to know their location? Do they fear people? Mary swears they turned to fright when they took notice of her back at camp.

And where the hell were her friends, assuming she could call them that? This girl's hole wasn't far from the tent, and yet she had not heard any voices beyond their own. Were the brothers still out in the woods looking for Julie? And what about Adam? He stormed off at some point before she and Justin got hot and heavy. Was he pouting somewhere? Maybe back in the Escalade?

"They want you."

Mary snaps out of her daze and meets the girl's gaze. "Huh?"

"The women in red. They're looking for you."

Mary doesn't know who she means. "Is that why we're here?" she asks.

"Partly."

Mary waits for more, but nothing comes. So, she asks, "Why do they want me?"

"They think you're the one from their premonition."

Mary is beyond confused. "What are you talking about?"

"They're raising one of their gods tonight. I've heard them talk about it. About Him. And about you. At least, they think it's you. It must be. I saw you fight that snake. Who else could it be?"

"What the hell are you talking about?"

"There's a girl they fear. And a story about their Higher Power killing the world... There's someone that can defeat then during the White Ritual. Whatever that is. They don't get many chances to do this. Not often, I don't think. Otherwise, why would we still be here? Of course, they want to get it right this time. I don't know how many times they've already tried and failed at this."

"A premonition?"

"Yes. I've heard pieces here and there. Some of the girls don't think their leader is taking it seriously enough. But there's traps everywhere."

"And there's someone they think can stop them?"

The girl nods.

Mary chuckles uncomfortably. "Why would that be me?"

The girl considers something, but her lips remain sealed.

Mary looks out the hole, up at the red sky overhead. "So, everything I've seen tonight has been real? I'm not just tripping on mushrooms?"

The girl shrugs. "Could be a bit of both. I don't know what you see."

"I see a red sky and a million eyes."

The girl nods sadly and wipes a tear streaking the dirt caked to her cheek. "You see what I see then. But I think those are isolated. Like, proximity to the mountain. Otherwise, the army would be here, don't you think?" She sniffles and rubs her cheek against her shoulder.

"Why are you crying?"

"My father."

"Is he here?"

"I think...he's one of them now."

"One of who?"

"The eyes."

Mary bites her lip and wonders what the girl means. Clearly, she's crazy. None of this night has made any sense. She's probably just dreaming, tucked away in a sleeping bag with Justin spooning her with his hard cock pressed against her ass. Wouldn't that be a way to wake in the morning? She smiles and the girl catches her.

"Why do you look *happy*?" she demands.

Mary wipes the smirk from her face and apologizes. "I was thinking of someone I came here with. I was just...daydreaming."

"Bury that shit. This mountain is part of an unholy ritual and you're over here drooling like a horny teenager."

"Excuse me, but aren't *you* a teenager?"

"Not anymore," the girl says, turning away again.

"Well, that settles that, I guess," Mary says with a sigh, picking at a loose thread on her shorts and rolling her eyes. "So, like...am I your prisoner or something?"

"No," the girl says, insulted and annoyed. "I'm trying to keep you safe."

"Then at least tell me your fucking name."

"Farrah."

"Oh. I like that. I'm Mary."

"I don't care. I just want to survive the night."

"Are we just going to hide until morning?"

Farrah turns and sets her back against the wall. Surprisingly, her muscles relax, and suddenly she appears smaller. Exhaling loudly, she closes her eyes and thinks for a moment before replying. "I don't know what we need to do. I'm just hoping you're the one they mentioned."

"What did their premonition say about me? Or *whoever*

can stop this."

"I don't know much else. That's the problem. I got the impression this group is still new. I don't know if they were even together the last time they tried this ritual, but... I know they're desperate to get it right. Their leader is a twisted bitch. She's the one that called the eyes to watch for you."

"The ones in the sky?"

"There, yeah, but also down here. I've seen the trees move. The vines and roots." She licks her lips and sniffles. "And whatever you do, avoid the clearings."

"Like our campsite?"

"Yeah. You're out in plain sight there. You need to be hidden, have the element of surprise." She runs a dirty arm across her nose and curses. "I found holes like this all over the mountain, you know. Caves and tunnels, too. I've been using them to hide while searching for you and keeping tabs on them."

"How long have you been out here on the mountain?"

"Four nights now, I think. My father and I came looking for truffles. After I lost him, I overheard a conversation between their leader and a follower, the one that is closest to her. I then found a cave with drawings on the walls and an altar of bones. I started following the group after that. I kept my distance and eavesdropped whenever I could. Sometimes, I lost track of them. As if they could just vanish into thin air. But there are several tunnels that connect back to their camps, so I would find them again later." She laughs dryly and looks away. "I listened to them and their craziness a lot those first two days. After what I'd already seen with my dad, I figured their babble was probably true. And I knew I couldn't leave the mountain after that. If I didn't find you, then their Higher Power would destroy everything. How could I just go home, pretend I didn't know there were devils on our doorstep? That would be like accepting the end of the world. I believe that now, after all I've seen and heard. Waiting for you to arrive seemed like my best option. I had hoped you'd be here sooner, but at least you came. Now you can put an end to all this."

"Did you ever try calling for help? The police?"

"My phone couldn't get a signal when it was working. It's been dead for a few days now."

Mary takes it all in as best she can and decides to play along for the time being, although she is thoroughly confused and overwhelmed by it all. "What if I'm not the one they're worried about?"

The girl visibly shudders. "Don't say that. If it's not you, then we are *all* fucked. Because I saw the twisters in the sky. I'm pretty sure I know what that means."

"That...they did it?"

Farrah nods. "They performed whatever ritual they had planned, and their demon is here."

"What does it look like?"

The girl smirks. "I think we will know it when we see It."

Though the orb's stalk is sensitive to Justin's grip, his throttling isn't enough for the creature to spit him out. He doesn't think they've really moved from their spot in the forest, but he does know they're still high above the ground. Even if he manages to open the monster's mouth, where would he go? Jumping from the treetops would be suicidal unless he climbs down. But wouldn't he be chased? Snatched from the earth and devoured again?

He has the dead man's gun in hand. He just needs to decide what to do with it. Shoot the orb? Its stalk? The creature's enormous jail-like teeth? He's even considered being swallowed on purpose, that way he can shoot through its belly or anus for a lower drop to the earth. The problem is the stomach acid; he has no idea how quickly it may burn him. Taking such a risk seems almost as stupid as jumping from the treetops.

The decision is made for him. The mouth tilts upward at a 90-degree angle, taking his feet off the creature's tongue and dangling him over its throat instead. Justin holds onto the stalk for dear life and struggles for a plan in the darkness. Though his eyes have adjusted a little since his capture, he still can't see much of anything.

As if to read his mind, the orb reignites so brilliantly that Justin is blinded and releases his grip on the stalk. Though the throat is wide, he falls in such a way that both his feet and head are making contact on either side of the esophagus. He's too tall to simply drop with ease. This allows him to straighten his spine as much as possible and get a grip halfway down the bastard's gullet.

Here, sticky with saliva and God knows what else, Justin wonders if he'll be able to shoot his way out through the neck without losing his traction and falling into the stomach. He can hear the hissing and popping of acid below, not far from him. He tries to imagine the monster as a potbellied giant, all midsection and short in limb. From his brief glimpse he had outside, Justin knows the head is mostly the mouth.

He thinks unhappily of the eyes above as he tries to work his finger over the revolver's trigger without relaxing his arm too much in the process. With all his might, he pushes himself outward from top to bottom to keep himself lodged in the throat.

"This is stupid," he grunts, exhausted already from the gravity weighing down on him.

If he shoots the gun, he'll just fall in the process. It's not like the monster's neck is going to explode and toss him out. The creature is standing vertically, not leaning forward at a helpful angle. He needs a new plan and fast.

A grumble rises from below him in the darkness of the hot pit. The creature is getting tired of this game. It tries swallowing harder, its throat constricting and forcing Justin to bend his arms and legs. After several attempts, the creature finally succeeds in knocking Justin loose from his purchase. He tumbles headfirst into the depths below and lands with a splash in the stomach acid that awaits him.

"There must be books, right?"

Farrah turns to Mary and asks, "To read?"

"Books from the cult. Like, of their spells and rituals."

"There's a journal their leader sometimes carries. I've never been able to get it for myself, though."

Mary fidgets with her hands and scratches the dirt from her palms. "We should look for it."

"Why?"

"Because it could explain something we need. It's not like I have any clue on how to fight their god. Do you?"

"I'm assuming it's something about you. Something natural."

Mary looks at her, confused. "You mean I don't have to *do* anything? Just by being near it, things will work out?"

Farrah shrugs and pokes her head outside the hole for a moment. When she returns, her face is speckled with water. "It's beginning to drizzle."

"There are clouds?"

Farrah simply shakes her head.

"I don't understand. If there aren't any clouds, where is the rain coming from?"

"Maybe the eyes," Farrah says, swallowing hard. "Maybe they're crying."

Mary studies the girl. Earlier, she'd said her father was possibly there, in the sky. What did she mean? Does she think the eyes are good? Everything inside of Mary tells her that the eyes are wrong, that they are *bad*.

"Why would they be crying?" she asks.

"Because they can't find you."

"I thought we didn't *want* them to find me..."

Farrah sniffles and wipes her damp face. Mary wonders if any of those so-called tears from the sky actually belong to the girl.

"I think they're torn between two worlds," Farrah says. "That they're just serving a master because they have no other choice."

"Sounds like life for us all," Mary snorts. She wants to leave the girl behind, even if that leaves Mary on her own. She's not sure she can really trust Farrah, not with this shit about her father being in the sky. At first, she thought maybe the girl would help her escape the mountain and this bizarre night. But now—she can't help but worry that Farrah will feed her to the demon god herself if she thinks it will somehow free her father.

"Where are you going?"

Mary comes out of her daze and realizes she's standing

as tall as the cave will allow. She appears ready to leave, though she doesn't remember making the decision to do so.

"I'm, uh...I'm going to find that journal you've seen."

"Where will you look, though?"

"Anywhere. My friends are out there, and I need to find them, too."

Farrah places herself in front of the exit, blocking Mary's only escape. "I think we should plan a bit first."

"Well, let's hear it then."

"You're the chosen one, as stupid as that sounds."

"So, you say."

"Maybe we should just follow the vortexes. Right to the source. If the journal is important, I bet it's with them there."

Mary nods and inches closer to the girl and her exit. "Makes enough sense. Let's go."

"Like this? Empty-handed?"

"No. We can get shit from camp first. I know we have some flare guns, at the very least."

This seems to relax Farrah, who steps aside. Mary climbs up from the hole and hurries into the surrounding brush to keep out of sight of the eyes searching above. For now, they haven't noticed her emergence. The young girl follows a second later and keeps hot on her heels. They make their way up the cliffside like this, always hidden, until they've reached the backside of the tent.

"Here goes nothing," Mary says, mostly to herself. She steps out into the clearing and hurries over to the bags near the fire. The one she overturned earlier is still spilled beside the tent, with nothing but clothes and packaged snacks to be found.

As soon as Mary is exposed from the brush, a great many

piercing screams bring her to her knees. She slams her palms over her ears and places her head against the dirt. Farrah appears beside her and immediately grabs her under the arm to pull her forward.

"What the hell are you doing?"

"Don't you hear them?"

Farrah scans the campsite, then looks up to the sky. "Hear what?"

"The eyes. They're screaming."

"I don't hear anything."

Mary lifts her head and removes her hands from her ears. The screaming has faded, but all the eyes are focused on them now. Farrah helps Mary to her feet and takes her to the remaining bags atop an overturned log. As Mary is lowered, Farrah notices the bite marks on her ankle and grabs her leg for a closer look.

"Why didn't you tell me about this?" Farrah demands.

Mary looks at her ankle and realizes it has blackened. Luckily, she can no longer feel any pain from it. "I actually forgot I was bit," she says, sweating. "It doesn't hurt like it did earlier, so who cares?"

"You don't look good, though," Farrah tells her. "Maybe you've been poisoned."

Mary pulls her leg away from the girl. "I can move, so let's forget about it."

"But your eyes..." Farrah looks at them close, grimacing. "You look intoxicated."

"I am," Mary grumbles, pulling one of the bags toward her to search. "The mushrooms, remember?"

Farrah studies her for a moment before shaking her head and joining the search.

As they dump the bags and sift through their contents,

Mary periodically glances toward the starlight glares. Occasionally, one screams shrilly in response to another. Farrah doesn't react to any of them. How can she not hear their calls? Is it because Mary's the "one" and Farrah is just some random teenager? Or is it because of the possible poison coursing through Mary's veins?

All of this is fucking nuts, she tells herself. *The eyes are a dream. The screams are a dream. Her "destiny" is a dream. It's gotta be.*

She collects two of the flare guns—slipping one into her back pocket and keeping the other ready—and discovers a knife to replace the one she used earlier on the snake. It's smaller and cheaper but should do the trick. She looks over to see Farrah's progress as she pockets the blade. The younger girl has found a small machete and removed its leather covering. She's currently examining it beside the fire, touching the blade to determine its sharpness.

"Looks new," Mary tells her. "Justin probably brought it for chopping up branches or something." She collects the third and final flare gun from the mess of supplies and hands it to Farrah.

"Thanks," the girl says distractedly.

The eyes start screaming again, shattering Mary's focus. She returns her hands to her ears and holds her chin tightly against her chest. Farrah watches her fearfully, then turns to the sky. She raises the gun and screams for them to stop. After a moment of hesitation, she decides to go ahead and fire the flare. It soars into the night sky and explodes as promised, but the eyes simply narrow in annoyance. Farrah tosses aside the empty gun and curses. As she goes to grab Mary from the ground, the trees opposite them begin to shudder.

"Why the fuck did you do that?" Mary demands.

"I was hoping it would hurt them or something," Farrah cries in frustration. "At the very least, it has signaled our location for help to arrive."

"Like the police? You think they can kill the demon instead?"

Farrah shakes her head. "No. But having someone come to our rescue is still better than having no one at all," she argues stubbornly.

Mary stands and turns toward the shaking trees. "Shit, there's so many of them!"

Farrah follows her gaze but sees nothing beyond the campsite. "What are you talking about? What do you see?"

For Mary, there's a tribe of naked goblins stepping out of the forest, armed and angry. They're holding wicked blades and nets in their hands. Every exposed dick is rigid and pointed like a spike in her direction. Their teeth are sticking out of their mouths at crooked angles, unbridled by their fat, red lips. Their bulbous eyes appear as crazed as they are hungry, some of which spiral within their sockets like spinning slot machines.

Farrah grabs Mary by the shirt and yanks hard on it. "Hey! Hey, what do you see?"

Mary raises her flare gun and takes aim. She's going to set them on fire and stop their advance before it's too late. Sweat is running down her face and from under her arms. She feels jittery and scared. Maybe Farrah is right about her being unwell. She shakes away the thought and puts her finger on the trigger.

"No, we can't waste another!" Farrah begins to yell, but it's too late. The trees opposite them catch fire from the flare and howl in pain. *This*, Farrah can hear, though she does not know why. Does that make it actually real, unlike whatever Mary has imagined?

"I fucking got them," Mary says, smiling victoriously. "Just give them a second to smolder before we move through them."

All Farrah can see are the trees burning and shuddering, as if in pain. Are they alive, like the ones she's seen move? To some extent, they seem to be.

"Who, Mary? Who did you get?" she asks. When she spots the rivers of sweat dripping off the girl, she curses. She is now sure that Mary has been poisoned and is quickly losing her grip on their already twisted reality.

"The goblins, of course," Mary tells her, running an arm across her brow. "And you're fuckin' welcome."

Farrah decides, *fuck this*, and yanks Mary by the hand toward the woods beyond the far side, away from the growing fire. "Let's just go. Come on."

Though the acid burns, Justin isn't dead or dying. Not yet, at least. He brings his head above water, so to speak, and sputters. What's gone down his throat has immediately made him gag; he begins to vomit into the surrounding pool until his eyes hurt. Once he's deposited all that he can, he checks his gun and curses. It's dripping in stomach acid—will it even work anymore?

Only one way to find out, he thinks, taking aim at the stomach wall opposite him and pulling the trigger. In the darkness of the beast, there's a brilliant flash of light as the weapon explodes in multiple directions. Though a bullet does appear to pierce the stomach wall—issuing a scream from the monster—the gun also sends hot pieces of shrapnel into Justin's face, temporarily blinding him. He drops the remains of the pistol and screams while clawing at his face. His skin is burned in multiple places and bleeding from several cuts, but he is otherwise okay. He blinks several times and tries wiping his face dry, but he's soaked all over.

"God damn it!" he screams, punctuating every word.

Thanks to this new injury, the beast seems to be stumbling around the woods in pain. Its screams shake the entire stomach, sending Justin up and under the acid repeatedly. Finally, he finds some sense of footing and moves toward the puncture he made in the beast with the pistol. It's small, but he can see moonlight—or is it the glare of a million eyes?—peeking through the hole. He sticks two fingers outside and does his best to widen the hole, twisting and finger blasting the beast with vigor. It screams and begins to run. Every step sends Justin several feet into the air, as if he's on a trampoline. Though this causes him to lose the hole again and again, he always returns to it; because that's what you do when you're finger blasting, right? You battle the bronco until it squeals and squirts.

Within a minute of his exercise, the hole is large enough for Justin to push the rest of his fist through. The beast crashes into a set of trees and doubles over in pain. For a moment, Justin catches a glimpse of the ground and the leaves covering its forest floor.

"Freedom," he says under his breath, momentarily forgetting the pain of his burning skin.

Justin punches through the bloody puncture once more, twisting his arm until he's screwed his entire limb up to the shoulder through the hole. Then he yanks himself back into the stomach and uses both of his hands to grip the wound and pull it wider. Acid is now flowing outside freely whenever the beast stumbles and the tide rises. Justin doesn't quit, though; he pulls and beats and sweats for that hole. The monster finally falls onto its side, screaming in death-throws. Justin works his head outside, then his shoulders. A minute later, he is birthed from the midsection of the beast and free of its leaking acid.

"YEAH! YEAH! FUCK YOU!" he howls at the dying animal, shaking his tattered clothing in a pointless attempt to dry off. The creature is large and has knocked over several trees in its fall. Justin stares at it for a long minute in horror, waiting to see if the image might fizzle, proving to him it was all a hallucination. But the creature remains, wheezing and deflating right before his eyes.

As Justin turns to leave, a dozen owls land on the branches of the surrounding trees in a flurry of startling movement. He pauses to gaze from one to the next. The owls are unusually big—as large as dogs—with shining eyes of silver that intensely focus on Justin.

"Shit..."

One of the owls swoops down from the tree with its claws outstretched before it. Justin throws up his arm in defense and feels searing pain as the owl's talons tear chunks of flesh from him. As it climbs higher, back into the trees with the others, Justin lowers his forearm to inspect the damage. The gashes are deep enough that he can see white.

"Motherfucker," he curses, turning to run.

The owls launch from the trees to give chase.

CHAPTER 7

PROTECTING THE ORDER AND LORD

There's a yellow path twisting through the woods. It shines like a spirit guide that only Mary can see. She leads the way as Farrah tries to keep up, repeatedly saying, "This is a bad idea," every time they take a sudden turn in the trees.

"I'm telling you, kid, I see it," Mary insists, chasing the yellow path like it's the rabbit from Wonderland.

"Don't call me kid!" Farrah growls. "I'm not that much younger than you." She looks over Mary's shoulder for the light but sees nothing. "I swear, you're imagining this shit!"

Mary stops hard and shoves Farrah back several feet. "I fucking see it, kid. You can either follow me or get fucked."

Farrah is surprised by the outburst and stutters in response.

Mary points behind her. "Something is taking me the right way. Am I the chosen one or not?"

"I hope so, but what the fuck do I know?"

"You're the one who told me I can stop this!"

Farrah licks her lips and realizes Mary's eyes have changed again. They're larger than they were at the campsite. Darker too. She looks more than intoxicated now; she looks *wild*. Even the veins in her neck are enlarged and prominent. "What's wrong with you?" Farrah asks.

Mary is grunting and sweating profusely. "What do you mean?"

Farrah looks around them and notices a garden of bioluminescent flowers at their feet. As she shifts her shoes in place, she spots spores dancing into the air. She looks again at Mary and notices the girl's nostrils flare as she breathes in the stuff.

"Shit. What is this?"

Mary looks down at the flowers and runs a foot through them, kicking up a cloud of spores in the process. "Pollen. Who cares?"

Farrah takes in a lungful and coughs. Within seconds, she feels different. She feels excited and full of energy. "I think it's something else," she says, purposefully taking another deep breath. Her body feels alive in a way she's never felt before. When she looks from the flowers to Mary, she can see her companion feels the same.

"Maybe we can take a short break," Mary says, sucking in the spores through her nose and licking her lips. She takes a step closer to Farrah and smells the side of her neck. "You smell *so* good. How do you taste?"

Farrah shakes her head and steps back. "We've got to go. We're wasting time."

Mary surprises them both by shoving Farrah to the ground and jumping on top of her. She brings a fist down into Farrah's face, breaking her nose and sending up a spurt of blood. Farrah gasps and throws her arms over her face for protection.

"What the fuck? Get off me!"

Mary continues to swing her hands and elbows down on the girl, screaming crazily all the while, "Kiss me! Kiss me!"

Farrah twists her body as hard as she can, knocking Mary off her just enough to get leverage. Farrah then quickly climbs onto the girl and shoves Mary's head into the ground with all her strength, stunning her for a second. Hoping that will be enough, Farrah jumps to her feet and turns to run. Mary immediately grabs her by the ankle and yanks her back down. Farrah's head hits the side of a log, and she sees stars. Once they've cleared enough for her to recover, she realizes Mary is disappearing into the woods, leaving her behind.

"No!" she screams after her. "Come back!"

But the "chosen one" is gone.

Mary picks herself up gingerly from the flowers and sneezes several times. As she rubs her itching eyes and groans from the knot on her head, there is movement from around her. She blinks back her tears and scans the area. After a minute of silence, she considers giving chase after Mary. Though she can no longer see the girl, Farrah is sure she will arrive at the fiery vortexes just the same if she follows the smoke and lights.

There is movement again to her left. She looks and swears a tree six feet away from her has shifted in place. There's a thicket at its base that also seems to squirm with anticipation. As Farrah watches it closely, holding her breath, she spots a vine stretching out from the brush and reaching toward her ankle.

It is time for her to leave.

———•———

The owls have chased Justin for several minutes by the time

he skids to a stop at the edge of a cliff. He can see a large shape below, moving and grunting, but cannot tell what it is in the darkness. He turns back to the trees as the owls land in the lowest hanging branches.

"Fuck off, will you?"

The owls screech at him and flap their wings. One swoops down and takes a bite out of Justin's ear as he dives to the ground. The pain is just one of many. He screams in frustration and punches at the bird. Its claws tear deep gashes into his forearm before returning to the trees. Blood splashes the surrounding leaves.

"You goddamn bird!"

Behind him, from the cliffside, he can hear something approaching. Every second, the ground shakes a little more. Justin glances over his shoulder, but there's only darkness for now.

What the hell is that?

The owls take flight and begin to circle overhead like vultures. Their eyes are glowing brighter now as they screech rhythmically, dipping up and down in a kaleidoscopic pattern.

"What the fu—"

Something growls from the cliffside, pulling his attention away from the birds. The thunderous sound is low and commanding. Justin gets to his feet and peeks over the ledge cautiously.

It gets better, he thinks with disdain.

Below, a large, scorched demon is climbing toward him.

Justin swallows hard. "Jesus, make this night end." He turns to run. He's barely returned to the trees when the demon climbs over the cliffside and stands. Justin slows to look back. The thing is at least fifteen feet tall and strapped with throbbing muscle. Grinning widely in Justin's direction through the cluster of trees, it snatches a handful of the owls from the air, shoves them crying into its mouth, and chews. Their bones snap with ease as its razor-sharp teeth grind the corpses to a pulp. Blood drips down the demon's chin as the others take flight above the trees, fleeing for safety.

Not for the first time, Justin damns himself for having taken mushrooms earlier. He has no idea whether he can trust his eyes; but after what he's been through tonight, he can't risk discounting them. And this thing—this fucking king demon of some kind—is far too dangerous to ignore.

So, he runs like hell.

Mary is chasing the yellow path as it continues to pulse one step ahead of her. The spores she breathed earlier have left her fuzzy around the edges, but she was under multiple influences already. Though her eyes are itchy and aching as she rushes through the woods, deeper still, she has energy coursing through her skeleton from the pollen that can only be good for what lies ahead.

Several minutes have passed before she realizes the feral girl is no longer behind her. She might be giving chase, but Mary isn't sure. She doesn't really care, either. To be rid of the twat is fine by her. Above all, she wants to locate her friends and get the fuck off the mountain. If there's a monster to slay in the process, so be it. Whatever gets her back in Justin's arms. Maybe he's with the vortexes, dancing naked, high off his ass. Maybe *all* of her friends are there, and the strange shit she's seen tonight can be written off as a wild trip. She can only hope.

Occasionally, a tree shifts in place, sometimes twisting in her direction. Mary does her best to ignore them as she pushes onward. She has the second flare gun if she needs it. But the fire she started at the campsite is raging like a perfect warning—*don't fuck with me, trees, or you're next*.

Maybe the fire will kill them all, she thinks, looking back the way she came. The glow is becoming increasingly bright, and there's smoke filling the sky, clouding the eyes from sight.

"Good," she says aloud. "Maybe they won't be able to see me coming then."

She quickens her pace.

The clearing. Farrah has stumbled upon it once more.

She skids to a stop and curses. How did she get here? Hadn't these sky straws been located elsewhere on the mountain? She scans the cursed space in search of her father's floating corpse, but he seems to be missing. So maybe this isn't the same spot as before. Maybe there are more. Whatever the case, she spots seven circles of light piercing through the treetops. She knows to avoid them. Did Mary come through here at all? She's not being sucked dry anywhere, so it seems she managed to skip it.

Did she really not come through here?

Farrah groans, taking a look at the sky where the smoke continues to rise. She's still headed in the right direction.

"What am I doing?" she asks herself after a minute of gazing into the eyes above. She lowers her chin and carefully crosses the clearing to the other side, thinking she needs to be more careful if she's to survive this hellish night.

She pauses mid-step as she nears the edge of the clearing.

She hears someone quickly approaching and wonders if it is Mary.

A man suddenly bursts from the trees and slams into her. The collision is hard enough to knock them both to the ground. Farrah loses her grip of the machete she retrieves from the camp as it is flung backwards several feet from her hand. There, on the ground, she realizes the forest floor is trembling with the stomping of something much larger than this boy. Something that is chasing him and getting closer.

As Farrah pushes the stunned guy off of her and stands, she recognizes him as the one Mary was fucking in the tent earlier. His name is Justin, she thinks. Tommy had been the younger of the brothers, not that it really mattered—they were just fodder for this mayhem.

Justin looks different from the last time she saw him. His skin is raw and split open in many places. There's blood and puss running down his arms. His shirt has a huge gash across it and his pants have ripped knees. His face is blistered in such a way that Farrah is reminded of Freddy Kruger.

"Jesus Fuck, what happened to you?" she blurts out without thinking.

Justin collects himself from the ground, snatches Farrah's fallen machete, and eyes the young girl as he stumbles backward on shaking legs. "Who the hell are you?"

"Woah, watch where you're—"

Justin trips on his tattered shoes and nearly falls into one of the sky straws behind him. Farrah quickly grabs his ankle as it kicks into the air and yanks him away from the circle. In her hands, some of his skin sloughs off. She gags and flings the bloody mess away from her. On his back beside the moonlit hazard, Justin screams in pain as he grabs his leg and holds it up for a closer look.

Feed the sky. Feed the sky.

The voices are in his head again. He shakes them away and curses.

The trees break open behind them and a frighteningly tall figure emerges. Farrah turns and immediately knows she's in the presence of the cult's god. The king demon. It has continued to grow since leaving the vortexes, now more than seventeen feet high. There was never any rush for this creature to catch the boy; it was just a game, one that would hopefully lead the unholy monster to the girl from the Crimson Highness's premonition. The one who needed to die above all others.

Farrah urges herself to move as the creature registers the scene before its enormous stature.

She looks back at Justin and yells, "RUN!" before taking off, back the way she came. She doesn't bother looking over her shoulder for the boy, because she can hear him panting behind her a second later. The thunderous steps of the demon quicken as it follows, shaking the surrounding woods with every step.

And just where the hell was the chosen one in all this?

The two fires have died down since the demon's baptism, but Mary recognizes them well enough for what they were. Near them, there are numerous hooded figures listening to a naked woman covered in paint. Off to the side is something akin to a man, but larger, keeping watch.

Now what?

All Mary has is a knife and a flare gun. She handles the knife and tries to decide how it feels in her hand.

No, this is crazy, she tells herself. *Sure, they look like a cult. But I can't just sneak up and attack people I don't know.*

She turns back to the trees in search of the younger girl. She is nowhere to be seen.

"Damn it. Where is that little bitch when you need her?"

She looks back toward the group and sees the guard has vanished. The naked woman is throwing on a robe now as the others march toward Mary.

She's been spotted.

Mary curses and turns to flee, but the guard is standing behind her, towering in height and girth. Instinctively, Mary drives the knife forward into the torpedo-shaped being. Though the blade pierces them, the guard doesn't seem phased by it in the least. Mary swallows hard and takes several steps back as fear clings to her heart.

"Is this *her*?" the painted woman asks on approach.

The guard shrugs and yanks free the bloody blade, letting it drop to the ground.

The painted woman—perhaps the leader?—grabs Mary by the shoulder and spins her around. She places two fingers against Mary's lips and gently glides them down the girl's chin and neck, all the while examining her eyes.

"What are you doing?" Mary asks, regrettably aroused.

The leader leans closer and kisses Mary deeply, slipping her tongue into Mary's mouth and probing every inch. She then pulls back and grimaces.

"Are you a virgin?"

Mary swallows, wanting more. Maybe the flowers still have some control over her primal instincts. Though her energy has diminished, she still feels jittery and hypersensitive.

"No," she replies, breathless.

Not anymore, she thinks.

"Then she isn't shit," the leader tells the guard, swiftly turning back to the fire pits. "Kill her."

Mary's heart leaps forward in her chest. She tries to run, but a large hand grabs her by the arm and throws her back ten feet. As she tries to stand, she remembers her final flare and yanks the gun out from her back pocket. The guard approaches quickly. She fires the flare into their chest, setting them on fire. As the behemoth roars in pain—flailing blindly and bleeding over the leaves of the forest floor—Mary dives past it to retrieve her fallen knife. She uses the blade to stick the behemoth multiple times around the ribs and backside as it flails around her in pain, blinded by the flames.

The robed women turn, surprised to see Mary has gotten the upper hand. She turns toward them and charges.

The leader holds out her hand and yells, "Stop!"

"I don't think so," Mary growls, launching herself onto the painted leader and stabbing her repeatedly in the gut. The woman screams and tries fighting back but Mary is in some sort of adrenaline-fueled overdrive; she hardly notices the others behind her, desperately trying to pull her away as she continues to plunge her bloody knife into the leader again and again.

"GET OFF HER!"

She is yanked backward a step, but only for a moment. She blindly slashes her blade at the other women until she is released. She then quickly lunges back on top of the redheaded woman bleeding to death on the ground, this time to finish the job.

"No!" someone screams from behind her.

Mary drives her knife into the leader's breast all the

same, but the woman manages to laugh in her face. So Mary rips free the blade with a grunt and drives it into the girl's temple instead, all the way to the hilt.

Finally, Mary is successfully yanked off the cult leader and dragged several feet away. As she struggles against those that hold her, a curved blade is shoved through her carotid artery and dragged roughly to her opposite ear, nearly removing Mary's head in the process.

The not-virgin is choking on her last breath as a girl with a partially shaved head wipes her bloodied blade clean with the hem of her robe. She can see how deeply she cut the girl and is proud of herself for finding such strength. Unfortunately, it is too late for the Crimson Highness and her guard. Ardere is still breathing, but just barely—she has a hunting knife sticking through her skull, for fuck's sake, thanks to the bitch shuddering at the girl's feet—and Massif has succumbed to multiple stab wounds and the flames of the flare.

Oculi Sectatores has just lost two of their best, one being her lover and their leader.

"Now what, Sian?" one of the Others asks her.

"We carry on," she replies without hesitation. Though she wishes to cry over her loss, she steels herself for the sake of the Others watching her. She had always been next in command. "Supposedly, there is someone on this mountain that can stop our Lord. And we cannot allow that to happen. So, we'll spread out and find her. Anyone that isn't with our cause must die. Got it?"

The girls respond in unison: "Yes, Your Highness."

Sian swallows any doubt she has and stands tall. She's in

charge now. Ardere may have gotten them this far, but it is she that must try taking the White Ritual to its bloody end, whatever the cost.

She can mourn later.

CHAPTER 8
TAKING SHIT TO THE PARKING LOT (A FINALE)

Justin's entire body is screaming. The burns have intensified since his escape from the belly of the beast, and it certainly doesn't help that the new girl stripped his ankle bare of its skin. And sure, she saved him from one of those levitation suckers, but still—couldn't she have grabbed his pants instead?

He also wonders who she is and where she came from. Can he trust her? Does such a thing even matter when you're simply running for your life? Following a kid through hell seems almost riskier than going it alone, though.

Justin reminds himself of the ugly car they parked beside at the bottom of the mountain. This girl probably came here before them. That strip of gravel is where they need to run—it's their ticket off this fucking mountain. As for the others, are they even alive? He doesn't want to think about it. His brother, for Christ's sake, is one of the missing. Justin will come back for them. But first, he needs to get help.

The girl ahead of him is fast. He is hardly able to keep

up with her as they dodge through trees and brush. Are they still being chased? He considers looking back but—

As if on the same wavelength, the girl asks, "Is it still following us?"

Justin risks a look, though it seems unnecessary considering the noise of trees snapping and bending behind them.

The demon is even taller than before. Has it ever *stopped* growing? And just how big is it going to get?

"What the fuck do we do?" he yells.

"Your girlfriend needs to fight it!"

Justin stumbles and nearly falls in surprise. What girlfriend? Does she mean Mary? How does she know of Mary?

"What are you talking about?" he asks.

"The girl you were fucking in your tent. She has to fight this thing!"

Justin shakes his head in confusion. Rather than respond with further questions, he tries his best to increase his speed. The shaking of the earth is intensifying, which means the demon is closer than before. They need to find their exit and fast.

"Do you know where we're going?" he calls to her.

"Downhill! Never up!"

Justin wants to laugh. *Very helpful*, he thinks.

Ahead, a set of trees suddenly slam against one another, blocking their path. The girl tries to hit her breaks, but she's going too fast. She smacks into the them with her arms crossed over her face at the last second. Justin, however, manages to slow down and skid to a halt before her fallen form. As he goes to pick her up, one of the trees leans forward and opens a mouth full of tiny, sharp teeth. Justin reacts instinctively and swings the machete he collected earlier from the girl. The blade swipes across the bark of the tree and draws blood. Before he can question such an injury, he quickly grabs the girl by her arm and pulls her up.

They look for an alternate path, but the demon has caught up to them. They turn to face it just as a large hand reaches for Justin. Again, he swings the machete in defense. The blade strikes the demon's wrist and lodges there, but the dark lord doesn't seem to care in the least. It laughs as its hand closes around Justin's torso and lifts him into the air.

Farrah can't stop cursing. Monstrous trees are to their back, and the king demon is standing at their front. She is armed with nothing to fight with, and Mary's lover has just been snatched into the air. What is she supposed to do?

"HELP!" Justin screams as the demon brings him toward its unhinged jaw.

There's nothing she *can* do to save him.

Justin is tossed into the demon's enormous mouth where he immediately scrambles to his feet and throws up his arms to keep the teeth from shutting him in. Farrah can't look. She turns back to the vicious trees and launches onto one of them, just barely missing its own mouth. As she scurries up its branches, the tree swings itself from side to side, hoping to toss her away. Farrah moves as quickly as she can, fighting to make her way to the opposite side without falling.

Behind her, the demon forces its jaw shut on Justin while he uselessly pleads for his life. He is quickly bent backwards as the pale monster forces its mouth shut. Justin's arms snap inward and his torso splits open like a microwaved burrito overflowing from its seams. Entrails dangle from the demon's lips as its bloody teeth finally interlock. It then rolls the boy's corpse around in its mouth, crushing and grinding the remains into a chewy mush before swallowing the load.

Branches from the surrounding trees act as arms, reaching for Farrah as she slips her way in and out of safety. Their claws scratch and cut her occasionally, but she hardly notices. Her eyes are on the prize beyond—she can see the parking lot and her father's ugly sedan. She needs to hurry and jump, but the drop is going to hurt; she's at least fifteen feet in the air.

Nearby, the king demon finishes its snack and lumbers toward the fighting trees. Just as Farrah jumps out of the mangling limbs, the dark lord grabs two of the trees and rips them out of the ground. They scream as they're tossed aside, making way for the demon to continue its chase.

Farrah hits the ground hard and feels her ankle roll and her wrist snap with an audible click. She cries out, but only for a second. She bites back the pain as best she can and runs crookedly toward the parking lot at the bottom of the hill. She is nearly to the gravel when a hand latches around her midsection. She screams and kicks, but the demon has caught her. She turns to see it laughing triumphantly as it lifts her over its head and cranks its neck back to playfully dip her into its mouth.

Flailing, Farrah beats on the fingers wrapped around her, all the while crying and screaming for help. Then she feels it—the fucker's teeth. They close around her kicking legs and yank down diagonally, tearing her limbs off midthigh. The pain is blinding. Farrah immediately feels the blood drain from her face as her body burns with shocking intensity.

Then something happens.

The demon begins to gag. It drops Farrah on top of her father's car where the wind is knocked out of her and the windshield splinters. She gasps for air as the dark lord claws at its throat and stumbles in place. Then it lurches forward, wrapping its arm around its stomach, and vomits all over Farrah and the parking lot. Farrah gasps for air and waves her arms in front of her face desperately but is unable to breathe through the thickness of the bile that is washing over her. The demon heaves and heaves and heaves until there's a pool of bodily remains and blood and acid drenching the immediate area. As it crumbles to its knees and howls hoarsely at the sky, Farrah chokes to death under the thick blanket of vomit weighing her down atop the car.

Moments later, her eyes roll to the back of their sockets and she stops struggling.

The king demon topples forward, crushing the Market's Escalade with a thunderous crash, and bubbling from head to toe as it begins melting into a gory, crimson slush.

EPILOGUE

THE MOUNTAIN SWALLOWS DEEP

Officer Reyes switches on the squad car's siren and increases their speed up the winding road. Beside him, his partner, Officer Salt, sticks his head out of the window for a better look at the burning mountaintop ahead as they come along another curve.

"Jesus, E. What the hell is going on up there?"

"We've got people in need," Reyes tells him. "You saw that flare. All the smoke. Let the firefighters worry about the mountain. We've got to find those campers."

Salt returns his head inside the vehicle. "How, though?"

Reyes keeps his mouth shut. The truth is he has no idea what they'll do once they've reached the fire. He hopes the survivors will be there waiting for rescue.

"Watch out!"

Reyes hits the brakes as five deer leap across the road and down the opposite hill, slipping and crashing through the brush as they frantically flee.

"Shit, that was close."

"Better keep our eyes open for more. The fire is going

to be driving them all down the mountain."

Reyes nods and accelerates once more.

Sian stands beside the tent that briefly housed two lovers only an hour earlier. From her vantage point, she can see the flashing lights of a squad car racing up the mountain road. Behind her, the fires have grown and spread throughout the forest. She instinctively knows their Ground Lord has fallen, thanks to the girl's poisonous blood. If only she and the Others had been there with the king to help guide Him.

A follower steps up beside Sian and stutters, "What now, Your Highness?"

"This isn't the first time a Ground Lord has fallen," she reminds her sisters. "Another will rise in His place when the time is right. But we must start over again. Elsewhere." She looks to the sky where millions of eyes are vibrating and closing the spaces between them. "Our Higher Power will provide, as always."

A much larger eye forms over the campsite, increasing in size as more and more of the surrounding eyes sink into it. Joining. Blending.

Sian meets its gaze and is temporarily paralyzed as a sea of images floods her mind.

She is being fed a new path, a new plan. Soon, her training as the new Crimson Highness will begin.

The Others step back and observe, patiently awaiting guidance.

When Sian is released, she appears exhausted but mindful. She looks toward the flashing siren lights and then the spreading fire. Approaching the flames, she shuts her eyes and leans forward to recite the ancient words shared to her by the Eye of Eyes. When she is finished, the fire responds.

The police will soon be stopped.

The squad car skids to an angled stop in the gravel, ten or so feet shy of a crushed Escalade and a crappy yellow sedan covered in blood and other shit Reyes cannot identify. Both officers climb out of their vehicle and hurry over to the girl missing most of her legs. As Reyes checks her pulse, Salt swings his flashlight across the scene. The substance that covers the vehicles and gravel is yellow, sticky, and disgusting. There's a large mound of something crimson and black poured over the front of the Escalade and stretching twenty feet ahead of it. He swears there are broken bones in the mix, as well as shredded strips of clothing.

"What the hell is all this?" he asks, taking a knee and dipping his hand into the gore.

"Fuck it, Mike. We've got to look for survivors," Reyes growls, leaving the dead girl's side. What the hell happened to her? How did she lose her fucking legs? It looks like they were torn off by force.

Up the hillside, a path stretches through the darkness. There are downed trees reaching up the mountainside, some torn out by their roots. The glow of the wild fire is approaching them, but from a half mile away. Maybe further.

Salt retrieves his hand from the sludge and examines it under his flashlight. "Jesus, E. I think this is... What's the word? *Genetic material?*"

"What?"

"I think it's someone's insides."

Reyes stomps over to his partner's side for a closer look. "There's too much of it to be some poor splattered bastard. Now, get the fuck up. We've got to find the others. There are two vehicles here. Surely, this girl wasn't the only camper."

Salt stands and radios dispatch as Reyes marches off into the woods. He can't make sense of the broken trees or the enormous divots in the ground every six feet or so. He looks back toward the parking lot where his partner is talking excitedly into his radio link. Then he brings his eyes back to the growing fire. He finds the lack of wildlife deeply disturbing—shouldn't they have seen a stampede of animals by now? Not just five deer on the way up?

Maybe they got out of Dodge while we were still below, he tells himself, not at all confident in the theory. *Maybe they were already gone from before...*

He swallows hard and scans the hillside. It's difficult to see in the darkness of it all, but he's desperate for movement. He calls out to the black, but nothing answers him. He's about to turn back to retrieve Salt when a silhouette catches his eye. He does a double-take and spots someone standing at the edge of the fire, unflinching. He waves his arms through the air and shouts, "Don't just stand there! Come on!"

The silhouette multiplies. Soon, there are seven standing at the edges of the rushing flames. They don't appear to be moving, just watching.

Reyes calls down to Salt to hurry the fuck up. As his partner begins to climb after him, Reyes pushes himself up the mountainside, toward the flames. He can hear Salt yelling for him to hang back and wait for the firefighters, but Reyes strangely feels possessed to rescue the idiots looking to burn alive in the approaching flames.

Reyes's feet move faster. He works harder up the incline, grabbing trees for purchase whenever necessary, even jumping forward at times, as if that will help get him to the campers any faster.

Finally, the fire is directly ahead of him. Salt is somewhere below still, no longer in sight. Smoke is embracing Reyes as he nears the backlit silhouettes. He can see the campers clearer now, despite the burning in his eyes; there's an older man, a teenage girl, and five young adults, two of which are female. Their eyes are black, and their lips are curled in wicked grins that somehow reach halfway up their faces.

Reyes stops short.

"What in the fuck?"

The youngest girl looks familiar.

He just saw her dead in the parking lot.

Reyes opens his mouth to scream, but the fire immediately rushes forward at an accelerated speed and engulfs them all.

Sian leaves the flames, uninjured. She moves to the center of the campsite and drops to her knees there with the Others surrounding her. Eyes closed, she draws a series of symbols in the dirt using her finger, all the while mumbling a new ritual beneath her breath. When she is finished, she takes her knife and swiftly cuts open each of her palms. As the blood pools in her hands, she brings them together in prayer, pressed against her lips.

For a moment, all is still. Her sisters watch silently, each holding their breath. Around them, the fire is quickly gathering, cutting off any means of escape.

Sian suddenly claps her hands together loudly and the dirt around them explodes into the air, as if swept away by a powerful wind. The symbols she drew remain in the hard ground, etched into the stone skull of the mountain. As they begin to glow, the Eye of Eyes watches on.

The campsite sinks into itself then, swallowing Sian and the Others like they were never there. As the group is moved elsewhere, unseen, the ground closes once more, leaving nothing behind but a tent and some bags, all of which will soon become ash.

STAY TUNED FOR THIS

BONUS CONTENT

Author's Sketch Gallery ... 129

Early Renditions of the Gaast Cover Spread ... 141

"Cave Drawings" (A Novelette from the Prelude Series, *The Crimson Highness*) ... 147

For additional bonus content—including "Waking the Mountain" (A Prelude to *Feed the Sky*) and "Women of the Woods" (A Deleted Sequence from *Feed the Sky*)—scan the following QR code to visit a secret page located our website:

AUTHOR'S SKETCH GALLERY

I am a shitty artist, but I've been practicing a variety of styles in my free time. While writing *Feed the Sky*, I drew some images after the process to show my designs (some lost and re-sketched) that were used for this series.

I drew multiple pieces that showcased eyes in the sky. This sketch isn't accurate to the story because these eyes here include gore. In the actual books, the eyes in the sky are ocular orbs without any attachments. At least, none that can be seen at the time of the Watching. In other words, I was just having fun when I drew this one.

I have drawn Ardere multiple times, but they've all been terrible. I am having a hell of a time getting myself comfortable with sketching bodies, so this portrait shot will have to do for the time being. Here, she is in her cloak. The scars up and down her neck are not shown here, probably because this sketch was done prior to those details being added in editing. The original manuscript for *Feed the Sky* did not have her covered in ritual scars because she didn't have much of a back story at the time. This book started as a standalone novella before an entire series formed around it in editing.

There was a time I was considering a sequence in which Tommy had an encounter with Julie after her death, right before his discovery of the tunnel. She was going to stumble through fire toward him with parts of her body missing. Obviously, that scene never made its way into the story, but I've thought of using the idea elsewhere in the series.

These were sketches done for the tunnel. There's a dried-out man in the upper left corner that I never ended up using. Next to it is a generic skull (yes, I know it sucks). The second row features the half-heads—I've drawn them many times, but I'm just going to include these two here. As you can see, they vary in style; one only features the lower jaw, while the other doesn't break away until the bridge of the nose. The idea of the half-heads is that they were all different in ways like this, though candles always rested within the mouths.

This design of Glum-Rum differs a bit from the final version in the story, though most of his descriptors aren't included in *Feed the Sky* since Justin is too busy being eaten by the big bastard. Instead, read "Waking the Mountain" for the details, which include tiny eyes, spiky scales, and webbed feet, which are not seen here in this early design. Though he is killed in *Feed the Sky*, Glum-Rum is likely to return in the prequel series to this trilogy.

When Mary and Farrah emerge from their hideout and return to the camp, Mary hallucinates an army of naked goblins. This guy is a cleaner version than what I really envisioned, which included bursting boils and filth dripping off their limbs.

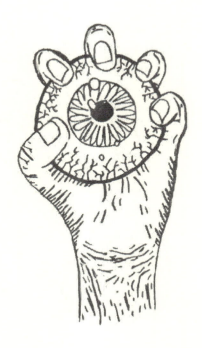

This is another generic design that really holds little connection to the story, beyond featuring an eyeball. Sometimes, I sketch stuff while writing that only shares in theme or mood, not actual substance. I have done a *lot* of eye sketches over the last few months preparing for this release. And yes, most of them are terrible. My hands shake throughout the day, so drawing perfect circles is nearly impossible for me.

There were several large sketches of the trees done before this one, but each of them was ruined when I attempted to color them in some way. This was the next best sketch that survived my experiments. Of those I ruined, gory limbs were included in the hands of the branches. This design doesn't even include hands or gnarled arms.

I attempted to draw the Justin-snake slithering out of Mary's vagina, but I could not get the legs right. She was supposed to be in a position to give birth but (as I mentioned earlier) I am terrible at drawing people's bodies and am still not ready to really show those kinds of sketches because of how embarrassingly bad they are. But I do like this alternate sketch of just the Justin-snake curled up in place. If you can't tell, I was imitating Jeff Lemire (*Sweet Tooth*, *Royal City*) with this one. I'm almost always imitating some artist in my sketches.

This attack spell wasn't included in *Feed the Sky,* but I plan to use it elsewhere in the series. Here, we have Ardere spewing sentient eyeballs from her mouth. If you've read *Cave Drawings* (featured in my *Nobody's Savior* collection), you know that one of these eyes visits the protagonist in that story. The spell itself will be directly detailed elsewhere in the prequel series, *The Crimson Highness.*

This demon design wasn't used in the end, but it could still appear elsewhere in the series. If it's not clear above, the head is meant to look very skeletal with eyes that sink into pits of darkness.

EARLY RENDITIONS OF THE GAAST COVER SPREAD

The following designs and sketches are early renditions of the cover spread that was used for this edition of *Feed the Sky*. The artist is the awesome Vlad Gaast, whose main links can be found below:

Instagram @v_gaast
Portfolio: industriacriativa.pt/rafael-sales
ArtStation.com/rsales

This was the first design concept for the front cover. The living trees surrounded the title text while the forest burned in the background.

This is the initial design again with some of the color added (not that you will be able to see the browns, greens, or yellows in this printing).

This is an early layout for what would become the final design for the front cover. Not shown here is a colored version that included cloudy energies surrounding the eyes. The coloring, in general, was different before Vlad went back to give it painted textures instead.

This is the first sketch for the back cover. The only changes that really came from this had to with the representation of the snake. Colors were changed when paint was added, and the face was made to look more human with stringy hair added in.

EARLY RENDITIONS OF THE GAAST COVER SPREAD

This back cover was originally colored with the snake looking more monstrous than human in the face. It did not yet have hair and was wearing a crown of thorns, which was removed from the final edit because it wasn't something from the story.

CAVE DRAWINGS

A Story from the Prelude Series, *The Crimson Highness*

1999

It was three weeks into the school year when Tara Wilkins started her new school in Virginia as a sophomore. She was shy and kept to herself. Except in homeroom, where she met a cute girl named Belle who went out of her way to talk to Tara. The two bonded fast and began seeking each other out in between classes and at the end of the day. But on the bus, she didn't ride with Belle—she rode with Kia and her asshole friends, all of whom began bullying Tara from day one.

The Wilkins house was set at the end of a long gravel driveway and surrounded by woods in every direction. The previous owners had made trails from their property by clearing dirt paths and nailing signs to the trees. Tara had always found herself most comfortable in nature, and was happy to at least have the woods to help her reset after a ride with Kia, especially since Kia had the same bus stop as she and would follow her part of the way home.

The driveway took five minutes to walk from the road. This gave her a chance to calm down enough that her father didn't know something was wrong when he saw her enter the house. Tara's mother wouldn't be home until several hours later and only spoke to her on the weekends. So, as long as she was able to fool her dad after school, her parents were none the wiser about her bully problem.

Belle told her to stand up to Kia more than once during that first month at Wellmount High. But Tara hated confrontation. Hell, she hated *general conversation* with most people. She wasn't the social type and never had been. She liked Belle, though. She liked Belle a lot, in fact. Sometimes, she'd stay up late in bed and wonder if Belle liked her the same way. She'd propose scenarios in her head in which they came out to one another. How well it could go.

Or how bad.

Tara's anxiety had kept her from making any sort of move on Belle, however tempted she was at times.

"As if being a dyke wasn't bad enough, she's also a nerdddd."

The mean girls cackled several seats behind her. Tara was doing her best to ignore them by reading a book during the bus ride home, but that had just given them additional ammunition against her. Someone flicked an eraser at the back of her head and laughed. Tara swallowed back her tears and refocused on the pages in her lap. Kia said something to her friends about Tara trying to lure her back to her place for some "dyke licking", but it was of course a lie. Tara's attraction was attached to personality, which Kia did not have. Tara thought of her as ugly, inside and out.

When they got off at their stop ten minutes later, Tara slipped her book back into her bag and tried to move down the road as fast as she could without running. Kia stepped off later than her and at a slower, more nonchalant pace—despite the bus driver telling her to "Hurry it up." As the yellow tube left them behind, Tara braced herself for what would surely come next.

"Wilkins!"

She didn't turn or acknowledge Kia. She quickened her pace and hoped to reach her driveway before Kia decided to move her own legs.

"Hey, bitch! I'm talking to you!"

Tara reached her driveway a moment later and turned onto its gravel. Kia laughed at her as she passed by, forever taunting Tara. A minute later, she was alone without another soul in sight. It was then she allowed the tears to come. But not for long. Once the house came into view through the trees, she took a tissue from her bag and wiped her face clear. Though her eyes were red, her father, Arnold, never looked too close at her whenever she returned home and hurried to the bathroom.

Through the door and from the kitchen, she heard him call out to her, "How was school?"

"The usual," she said, washing her face and checking her eyes. They still looked a little strained, but she had an idea if anyone asked.

She left the bathroom a minute later and took her bag to her bedroom. Her father appeared in the open doorway seconds behind her and said, "Dinner is going to be pizza tonight. Your mother is picking it up on her way home."

Tara nodded as she pulled out her textbooks to check over her homework. Most of it was already done, but she was doing this as a signal for her father to let her be.

"You okay?" he asked. "There's some bad juju floating around you right now."

She cursed herself for having not hid her mood better. "I'm just stressed out," she said. "I've got an assignment I'm dreading."

"What is it?" he asked.

"It's a paper," she lied, "about what we did over the summer. It has to be three pages long."

"What's wrong with that? I'm sure you can fill three pages easily. You were doing a lot during our last month in PA."

"I know, but..."

She hesitated as he watched her.

"I try not to think about all that," she mumbled.

"How come?"

She looked at him, anger surging. "Because you guys made me leave everyone behind."

He tilted his head a little as he took notice of her eyes. "Have you been crying?"

She looked away from him. "No. I have allergies here."

"That comes with changing states, usually," he said, entering the room and pulling her in for an awkward hug. "I'm sorry, kiddo. About the move. But we're doing so much better financially because of it. College will be easier now for us. High school...doesn't matter. I don't mean this to sound shitty, but these aren't friends you'll likely see much after graduation. That's just how it usually goes."

"I miss them," Tara said, trying to keep the tears from returning.

"I know, sweetie. And I don't blame you. My friends did a number on me after school ended. They all vanished, no matter how hard I tried to keep in contact. It's best to just be prepared for it now. Don't get too attached."

"But *they* didn't vanish. *I* did. Because of Mom."

Her father stepped back from her and nodded sadly. "What about Belle?"

"What about her?"

"Aren't you two getting close?"

She shrugged. "Yeah, I guess."

"Why don't you have her over for dinner sometime?"

Tara shrugged again, looking down at her textbooks.

After a few awkward moments of shuffling back and forth, her father took the hint. "Well, just let us know. I'll leave you to do your homework."

Once he'd left her room, Tara moved to her desk and turned on her computer. While it booted up, she looked at the wall covered in polaroids of her and her friends from back in Pennsylvania, including Jean. They'd finally shared a kiss as she was leaving. Tara hated herself for having waited until the last possible minute to make her move.

That wouldn't happen again.

Maybe dinner with Belle wasn't such a bad idea after all.

The next day, Tara found Belle in the hallway on her way to lunch and asked when she'd be available to have dinner at her house.

"Really?" Belle asked, smiling.

"Yeah. If you want." Tara shrugged, awkward. She felt exposed and vulnerable in a way she hadn't felt since saying goodbye to Jean.

"Okay. Um... I'll ask my parents and let you know."

Tara pulled a small piece of folded paper from her

pocket and passed it over. "That's our phone number. You can give it a call when you know what day."

Belle took the paper and smiled down at it.

"I have to get to lunch," Tara said, not knowing where to look as she stood there shuffling her feet. "I'll talk to you later?"

"Definitely."

As Tara turned away from Belle and hurried down the hall, she felt her heart racing.

After school, Tara used her portable CD player and headphones to tune out Kia and her friends on the bus. During the walk home, she continued to ignore Kia and didn't once look over her shoulder to see what the girl was doing behind her back. Tara was in such a good mood that she decided to explore the woods after dropping off her things inside the house and telling her father she was going out for a bit. He told her to watch the sky because a storm was coming, but she didn't care.

She'd yet to go off-trail, and decided to do so while she was feeling invigorated. Though it didn't take long for a drizzle of rain to start, the trees overhead kept the majority of it from really reaching her. The sound, however, had an intense calming effect on her. She went from bursting with energy to something more gel-like. More than once, she stopped to sit on a log and close her eyes. Minutes would fly by and, before she knew it, she'd been gone an hour.

She was about to turn back and return home—the rain was now falling heavier than before and she was getting wet—but she thought she heard something like a babbling brook nearby. She followed the sound as best she could through the rain, and a minute later she discovered the source. The waterfall was small, only ten feet above a pool of water that branched out into a thin stream through the woods, opposite the direction of her house. Tara watched it for several minutes, trying to decide how she could mark her way to it in the future, making it easier to find again. She had nothing on her person and wasn't entirely sure how far from the trail she'd gone.

She was about to turn back when a flicker of light through the waterfall made her stop. She moved closer and cursed under her breath.

"Fire?"

She needed to do something. She couldn't let it spread. But wait.

How was there a fire through the waterfall?

Tara walked around the side of the pool to the curtain and stepped through it, drenching herself in the process. On the other side was a cave with low ceilings and a thin birth. She ducked her head and moved toward the flickering flame ahead of her. It became apparent the flame was that of a torch someone had placed on the cave floor.

Shit, she thought. *I'm not alone.*

Turning fast to leave, she paused when something along the wall caught her eye. She leaned in for a closer look and realized someone had painted a picture near the cave entrance. A large eye was the focal point, and it was surrounded by stars with small trees and stick figures below. Tara shook her head curiously and stepped back out of the cave, into the rain. She found her way to the trail and followed it at a brisk pace, eager to return home.

She prayed no one was watching her.

"Where the hell have you been?" her father demanded as she stepped inside through the back door and searched for a towel above the washing machine.

"Sorry, Dad," she said, wanting to strip out of her wet clothes but waiting for him to leave the laundry room.

"You scared me," he said, his voice laced with anger and worry. "I tried yelling for you. How far did you go?"

She considered telling him about the waterfall, but the torch made her hesitant to do so. "I was just exploring and enjoying the rain," she told him. "You know it calms me."

He opened his mouth to say more, but then thought better of it. As he turned to leave her dripping on the floor, he asked if she was okay.

"Yeah," she said, nodding. "I had a good day. And the woods were very peaceful. I...uh... I needed it."

"You were resetting?"

She nodded.

He thought for a moment, still half-turned away from her. "I'm...going to get some long-range walkie-talkies for us, I think. That way you can keep in contact when you do this sort of thing."

"That would be good," Tara said, trying to smile.

Her father returned it and walked away. "Get in the shower before your mom gets home."

Once he was gone, Tara closed the laundry room door and pulled off her wet clothes. Once they were in the washing machine, she wrapped the towel tightly under her armpits and left for the bathroom upstairs, just outside her bedroom. As she showered, she thought of the waterfall and how she wanted to look for it again soon. Then she thought of taking Belle there by the pool and having a picnic.

For the twentieth time that day, her heart began to flutter.

The phone rang around seven, soon after they'd finished eating dinner. Her mother answered the call and yelled upstairs for Tara.

Though she'd only given their number to one person, she asked her mother who it was out of habit as she barreled down the stairs.

"Someone named Belle," her mother said, passing the phone with a yawn.

Tara took the phone and wandered out of the kitchen and into the den on the opposite side of the house. "Hello?"

"Hey. It's Belle."

She couldn't help but smile, and it sounded in her voice. "Hi."

"I asked my parents about dinner. They said I could come Friday night."

"Let me make sure with my dad real quick if that will work. Hold on a sec." She lowered the phone and covered the mouthpiece. She rounded the house to her father's office and pushed open his parted door. "Dad?"

Her father was sitting at his easel painting as Beethoven played from a nearby stereo. He swiveled around in his stool to look at her. "Huh?"

"Will Friday be okay to have Belle over for dinner?"

"Yeah, sure. Tell your mother." He swiveled back and returned to work.

Tara bit her lip and left the office. She hated going to her mother for anything. Planning dinner with her was near impossible.

"Mom?" she called out, not quite sure where to find her.

"What?"

Tara followed her mother's voice into the living room where she found her on the couch reading a book. "Dad said my friend could come to dinner and her parents said Friday would be okay. He told me to pass it on to you."

"Friday? I'm leaving for that weekend trip for work."

"So, you won't be here at all?"

"I wasn't planning on it. I was going to bring my suitcase with me when I left in the morning."

"Can Belle still come over, though?"

Her mother shrugged and continued reading her book. "As long as your father knows dinner is up to him to figure out."

Tara returned to the den. She had no intention of going back to her father once more. If push came to shove, she had money she could use to buy them takeout for Friday night. She uncovered the phone once she was a safe distance from her mother and said, "You still there?"

"Yeah, I'm here."

"Friday will be good. I don't know what we'll be eating, but we'll figure it out before then."

"Great! What time should I come?"

"We eat at kinda random times. When do *you* usually have dinner?"

"Like, six."

"I guess come around then."

"Okay."

Tara could hear the smile in Belle's voice as well.

"I'll see you then," she said.

Once they were off the phone, Tara returned the handheld to its cradle and hurried upstairs. She tossed herself onto her bed with a giddy laugh and pulled her homework close to her.

It had been a good day.

It was a little after two a.m. when the thunder woke her from an intense dream involving Belle. She sat up in bed and pulled back the curtains from her window to look outside. The sky flashed with lightning as rain pelted her window. She turned the security latches and lifted the pane several inches to let in the sound of the rain splattering against the frame. As she took the curtain in her hand once more to close it over the window, a shape outside startled her. She looked down toward the yard where a figure was standing outside the woods. When the lightning flashed, she saw it was a woman with long, red hair. Stranger yet was the fact that she appeared to be naked and covered in mud.

Tara jumped out of bed and hurried downstairs in her pajamas. By the time she'd reached the back door and thrown it open, the yard was empty. She looked for the woman, but saw no one standing in the rain. Had she imagined it? She waited several minutes for anything to change, but the storm was all there was to see. So, she turned back inside, locked the door, and returned to bed. It must have been part of her dream. As a toddler, she'd suffered from waking nightmares on a regular basis. Could it be that they were returning?

She checked the window one last time before shutting the curtain. Then she rested her head back down on her pillow and fell asleep to the sound of the pouring rain.

It was a miserable Thursday. Since getting up late for school that morning, Tara had run into one problem after another. First, she missed the school bus and had to ask her father for a ride. Then she realized she'd left her homework on the bedroom floor somewhere. After several classes of looking for Belle, she came to the conclusion that the only friend she had was out sick or avoiding her. Overwhelmed, Tara spent her lunch period in the bathroom hiding out in a stall and crying.

Class wasn't any better. She had trouble focusing because she felt exhausted, despite having had a normal night of sleep. The storm and the dream of the woman had only taken fifteen minutes from her—otherwise, she'd slept just fine. So, why did she feel like days had gone by without rest? More than once, teachers grumbled at her to wake up or pay attention. By the time the school day was over and she was getting on the bus, Tara was reaching a breaking point. To keep Kia from pushing her over the edge, she searched her pack for her CD player, only to find it was missing. She pressed her bag to her mouth and screamed into it. Several students turned to look at her with raised eyebrows, but she ignored them and scooted towards the window.

Somewhere along the drive, she fell asleep. When it was time for her to get off the bus, the driver had to leave their seat to shake her awake. They weren't happy to do it, either. Tara apologized, gathered her things, and got off the bus. Kia was ahead of her for once and waiting for her to catch up. As the bus left them behind, Kia smacked Tara across the back of the head as she was passing her.

"Wake the fuck up, moron."

Tara stopped in her tracks and turned hard on Kia. It was enough to make the girl stop as well, surprised by the look on Tara's face.

"Leave me the fuck alone, you ugly cunt," Tara spat, her nostrils flaring. "Touch me again and I'll fucking tear you apart."

Kia's mouth opened but nothing came out.

Tara turned back around and hurried to her driveway without looking back. Once she was home and inside the house, she kicked off her shoes—watching them smack into the wall hard—and stomped upstairs. She had never felt an emotion overwhelm her in such a way before. Though the outburst scared her, it also made her feel invincible. Like she no longer had to worry about Kia and her shitty friends.

Her father must have been too busy painting because he didn't come check up on her after she stormed through the house. Tara was happy to have been left alone. And instead of doing her homework, she climbed into bed and fell fast asleep.

Something made her stir. A presence. The kind of feeling you get when someone is standing over you.

Tara opened her eyes and closed them several times before realizing there was indeed something hovering over her bed. Startled, she shot up into a seated position and backed herself against the wall. A foot across from her was what appeared to be a detached eyeball, stalk and all, encased in blue fire. When Tara opened her mouth to scream, it launched forward through the air and dove into her throat. She choked, but only for a second—the eyeball slithered itself down into her intestines with surprising ease. Within seconds, she could no longer feel it squirming its way deeper inside her, like a nestling rabbit in its burrow.

"What the hell was that?" She looked around the room and rubbed a hand down her face. Had she imagined it? It'd happened so fast. It must have been a vivid hallucination and nothing more.

"Jesus, I'm losing it," she whined, feeling her anxiety rushing back to her as it had during school.

She tried lying back down, but realized her window was still open from the night before. When she moved to shut it, she saw that the screen had been torn open.

No, not torn—*burned*.

And the hole was just about the size of the eyeball she'd imagined.

Tara half-expected to see the girl outside again, but the yard was empty and the night sky was clear. Shutting the window, and closing the curtains, she checked the time. It was almost midnight and she'd never done her homework. Frustrated, she found her bag and pulled out her things to get it done.

She finished an hour later and found her mouth so dry that she felt like she was choking on her tongue. So, she went downstairs for water, and stopped dead when she saw muddy footprints moving from the kitchen door and into the bathroom. She followed them and stopped outside the door. From the crack, she could tell the lights were on inside. Was it her mother or father? Why had they gone outside barefoot and tracked in mud?

"Hello?" she said, tapping her fingertips against the bathroom door.

The crack went dark as if the light had been shut off. Tara took a step back, expecting whoever was inside to come out. But after several seconds of silence, it seemed that no one was leaving. She tapped the door again and listened close.

Someone was whispering in quick bursts, but too hushed for her to understand them.

Tara tapped once more and said, "What are you doing in there?"

The whispering stopped. Something crinkled and then there was silence.

Tara held her breath without realizing it. Her heart was racing, as if to tell her something was very wrong.

After a moment of hesitation, she reached out and opened the door. Stepped inside and flicked on the light.

The footprints crossed one another in the bathroom, but there was no one inside. Unless...

The shower curtain was pulled shut.

Tara took a shuddering breath upon realizing she'd held it in for so long. Then she pulled back the curtain.

The shower was empty.

"What the hell?"

She was about to leave when she noticed there were footprints in the shower as well. And they'd stopped at the back wall, as if someone had stood there and stared at it.

Freaked out, Tara hurried out of the bathroom and checked the kitchen door. It was locked. Then, just in case, she checked all the other doors to the outside. None of them were open or had been tampered with.

She ambled back to the kitchen and stuck her head inside. The muddy footprints were fading fast before her eyes. Within seconds, they had vanished.

Shaking in fear, Tara said a prayer to a god she didn't believe in, and hurried back upstairs to bed.

Her waking nightmares had returned.

It was finally Friday, which meant Tara was supposed to be seeing Belle for dinner. But again, she was not at school. Tara had looked for her numerous times throughout the day, and even asked people she knew had class with Belle to see if they'd heard from her. Without her friend, Tara sank into herself and was swallowed by darkness for the rest of school. She moved from class to class in a daze, shut inside her mind and ignoring everything around her. It was the only way to keep herself from crying. She needed to lock her mind and turn off.

On the bus ride home, Kia and her friends ignored her. Tara looked their way on two different occasions during the drive to see if they were doing or saying anything, but Kia always avoided her gaze as soon as Tara turned. Facing forward, she couldn't help but grin. *Thank God for small mercies*, she thought. *I guess I really scared her yesterday.*

When it came time to get off the bus, Tara got herself together with slow purpose so that Kia would be ahead of her during the walk. As they headed down the road, she felt a strange urge from within her gut to shout at Kia and taunt her the way she'd been doing to Tara since day one. It was unlike her and bewildering, but too strong an impulse to ignore the entire way. Though she did manage to seal her lips for most of the walk, Tara began to yell before turning down her driveway.

"That's what I thought, bitch!"

Kia's shoulders twitched upward, then fell. She didn't turn or say a word in response. Tara couldn't believe it. Seconds later, they were out of sight of one another.

I guess I took care of that problem, she thought. *Who thought it would be so easy?*

She neared the house several minutes later with her gut settled and her sadness returning. Would she be seeing Belle tonight still or was their plan canceled? Seeing as her friend had missed the last two days of school, it seemed like dinner wasn't happening. Tara squeezed her eyes shut in frustration and entered the house, ready to scream again.

Why didn't I write down her number? she demanded of herself. *Idiot!*

She had no way to call Belle and it was the weekend, so she would have to wait until at least Monday to talk with her.

Tara tossed her things into her room and switched from her shoes to her boots. The sky was clouded and growing dark outside, promising rain, so she located her slicker from the closet as well. As she returned downstairs, her father left his office to see why she was stomping about the house so much.

"I don't think Belle is coming for dinner," she told him as she fought back the sting in her eyes. "I'm going into the woods to cool down."

"Well, hold on then," her father said, disappearing around the corner once more. When he returned, he had a walkie-talkie that he handed to Tara. "Keep this on you, so we don't have any repeats of the other day."

"Alright."

He showed her how to use it, then asked, "Did something happen between you and Belle?"

"I don't think so. She's just been out of school the last couple days and I haven't heard from her."

"I see," her father said with a nod. "Well, I'll radio you

if she calls. Okay?"

"If she does, please write down her number."

Her father said he would and kissed her on the forehead. Tara thanked him and headed outside, feeling hopeful Belle might still call, even if it was to say she couldn't make it for dinner. At least, Tara would end up with her number.

She hadn't gone more than a few minutes from the house when her father called her on the walkie-talkie, "Looks like rain out there. Over."

She giggled, her mood improving a little as she slipped between the trees and found the trail. "That's fine by me," she replied into the handheld.

"You didn't say *over*. Over."

"No, no, no. Not this bit."

"Fine... Over."

Tara smiled and shook her head as she clipped the walkie-talkie to the side of her belt.

For a while, she followed the trail in a daze while thinking of Belle. Before long, she was returned to reality by the arrival of rain, which prompted a new scenario in her mind in which she and Belle were caught in the rain in each other's arms.

Stop that, she told herself, stomping her right foot as she walked in punctuation. *She probably doesn't like you like that.*

Upset with herself and her yearning for something she had yet to have, Tara branched off the trail and began jogging deeper into the trees, wanting to get lost. Wanting to disappear and be unreachable, at least for some time to escape her own torturous thoughts.

As she tired, she found herself in a small clearing where

the rain seemed to fall harder because of the increased crown shyness overhead. She paused and looked around herself. The trees surrounding the clearing were marked with carvings of eyes that seemed to study her. They ranged in size—some as small as silver dollars, others as large as steering wheels—and covered the trees from root to six feet or so.

Tara shivered at the sight. *What the hell?*

She approached a tree with a large eye at her chest level, and brushed her wet fingertips across it. She wasn't sure what she was expecting but the eye felt like a series of carved grooves in wood, nothing special. But as she took her hand back from it, the image glowed from the inside out, like a Jack-o'-lantern. Tara stumbled back in surprise and watched wide-eyed as the carving produced flames along its etched lines. Then, one by one, all the other eyes began to do the same.

Tara thought of her walkie-talkie, and unclipped it from her belt. She tried calling for her dad, but there was no response. Would the fire spread? As unbelievable as it seemed, the flames were only leaping from the outlines of the eyes, not running up the bark of the tree or leaping across branches. They didn't seem to show any interest in building or expanding. Instead, they simply pulsed in place.

Tara turned and ran from the clearing without making sure she was headed in the right direction. As she started through the trees, slipping occasionally on the wet leaves and even falling twice, the rain fell harder and louder.

She looked back—for what or who, she did not know—just as the ground was vanishing from beneath her. Suddenly, she was falling, but only for a second. Water swallowed her whole, and she began to panic. She kicked her legs—wild and fast—and threw up her arms. Once she'd managed to get her head above water and gasp for breath, she realized she was swimming in the plunge pool of the waterfall. She must have leaped off the ledge without seeing it coming.

Her panic began to subside as she took in her location. What were the odds she'd stumble upon this place again without having sought it out? A chill raced down her spine at the thought. In her mind, glowing eyes levitated in darkness, watching her. She shook away the image and shivered as she swam across the cold water toward the rocks and dirt.

When she climbed out of the water and stood, she checked herself for the walkie-talkie to make sure she still had it, and found that she did. But would it still work? She unclipped it to try radioing her father. Nothing happened.

"Shit, shit, shit."

She put the handheld back on her belt and told herself it was time to go home before her father lost it.

But first...

She turned toward the mouth of the cave to see if it was illuminated the way it had been during her last visit. This time, the cave appeared dark. Through the water, it was almost invisible. She moved towards it for a closer look and spotted a shirt on the ground at the edge of the entrance. It was once white, but now stained with dirt.

Someone must be living out here, she decided. After all she'd seen, how could she not assume there was a drifter in the woods? She hoped they were harmless, but...

The other night. The footprints into the bathroom. The naked woman she'd seen through the window. The carvings in the trees. Was this all the work of one person or several? She prayed there was only one of them. That was an easier pill to swallow than a group of drifters camping within walking distance of her house. Was this still their property? She doubted it. But if it wasn't theirs, who did these woods belong to? The city?

She shook her head and turned away. It didn't matter. She needed to get home.

"I'm sorry, Dad."

Her father swiveled in his desk chair to look at her. "For what? And where are your clothes?"

Before finding him in his office, Tara had stripped out of her soaked clothes and wrapped herself in a towel from the laundry room. She was desperate to get upstairs and dry off, but she figured her father would follow her up if she didn't swing by his office first.

"I fell," she told him, handing over the walkie-talkie he'd given her. "Into water. I don't know if it works anymore."

Her father took the handheld and tested it out. "I'll try putting it in rice or something."

"Okay."

She turned to leave, but he asked, "You fell into the water?"

"There's a waterfall in the woods," she explained. "And I didn't see it. I went right over the edge."

Her father's eyes widened as he stood to look her over. "Are you okay? How high was it?"

"Maybe ten feet. I'm not hurt or anything. Just soaked."

"Well, go warm up and dry off. Come talk to me once you've done that."

She nodded and left him to return upstairs. Ten

minutes later, she was on her back when she heard the phone ringing in the kitchen. She hurried to it and answered, "Hello?"

"Tara, is that you?"

Belle! "Yes. It's me. Um, where have you been?" She tried to hide the excitement in her voice and failed. She scrambled for a pad of paper and a pen to write down Belle's phone number.

"Sick, unfortunately. I won't be coming tonight. I'm sorry I didn't call sooner but I've been asleep for hours."

"It's fine. I figured you were going to cancel since you missed school."

"I'm really sorry. I really wanted to come."

"We can reschedule for next week sometime."

"I hope so."

"Did you, uh...want to hang out this weekend at all? Go to the mall or something?"

"If I feel well enough, I can call and let you know," Belle told her. "But at this moment, I'm still feeling miserable."

"What do you have?"

"I haven't been to the doctor. We can't afford to go...but I think it might strep. Hard to say, because sore throats can come with nasty colds, too."

"Your voice sounds normal enough, so hopefully that means it isn't strep. That shit sucks."

"I agree. I think it's just a bad cold, but it's really hanging on."

"I've missed you at school," Tara blurted before Belle's mouth had even shut. She squeezed her eyes shut and stomped her right foot three times.

"What was that sound?" Belle asked.

"Oh, uh, nothing."

"Well, I've missed you, too."

"Really?"

Belle's voice changed at this point. She sounded nervous and hesitant to reply. "Um, yeah."

Tara tried to move the conversation along without lingering too much on the admission that'd made her heart flutter. "So, uh, what have you been doing the last two days? Just sleeping?"

"Mostly. A little reading. And watching *Buffy the Vampire Slayer*, too."

"I've seen that before but haven't, like, watched it in order or nothing."

"I should fix that with you."

Tara smiled. "Promise?"

"Absolutely." It was clear Belle was smiling, too, from the sound of her voice.

"Tara!" It was her father calling for her from his office.

"Damn it," Tara said. "I have to go," she told Belle.

"No problem. I'll call if I feel better this weekend."

"I hope you do. Feel better, I mean."

Belle laughed. "Thanks. Talk to you later."

"Bye."

Tara hung up the phone and left the kitchen. When she entered her father's office, he turned around to face her. "Were you on the phone or did it only ring twice?"

"I got it. Belle called."

"Oh, good. How is she?"

"Sick."

"That sucks. We can get her over next week sometime."

"Thanks."

"Now, back to the waterfall."

"Okay."

"Where is it?"

"Uh... I don't really know. It's not along the trail. I found it both times by accident."

"*Both* times?"

"Yeah. I stumbled across it earlier this week."

"But you don't know where it is in relation to the trail."

Tara shook her head.

"Okay...well, I've got the walkie-talkie in a bag of rice. We can try it out tomorrow sometime. What are we doing for dinner tonight now that it's just you and me?"

"I don't know. I'm not very hungry, to be honest."

Her father nodded and touched a hand to his stomach. "Yeah, I'm not either."

"So, I guess we'll just snack whenever."

"Works for me, I guess. Hey, did you want to watch a movie later?"

"Sure. Let me know when you're done in here."

Once upstairs, she locked her bedroom door behind her and crawled into bed to read a book. Thoughts of Belle crashed over one another in her head, though, making the pit of her stomach warm with anticipation. She was too distracted to read, so she tossed her novel aside and grabbed a sketchpad from inside her nightstand instead. Like her father, Tara enjoyed drawing, though she was nowhere near as good as her father was at her age. She'd only started teaching herself a few months earlier, with the help of books from her school library.

Before long, she was drawing Belle submerged in the plunge pool of the waterfall with her portable CD player beside her.

Something was wrong. That's all she knew when she opened her eyes in the middle of the night, hours after watching a movie with her father.

She was itchy. And tickled. How was she being tickled?

As she blinked and sat up in the darkness, she fumbled for the lamp switch beside her. When the room illuminated a second later, she began to scream. Her bed and body were covered in tiny spiders. There had to be dozens of them, maybe even hundreds.

Her father bounded up the stairs and threw open her door a moment later. "What? What is it?"

Then he saw the spiders.

Tara jumped out of bed and began knocking as many off her as she could. Her father joined in, swiping them off her and smashing as many of them under his slippers as he could. Tara continued to cry and scream, shaking in terror. Her father swiped and smacked at her, before saying, "Just get in the shower! Quick! Wash them off if there are any in your hair or somewhere."

Tara ran into the hall to the bathroom, slamming the door shut behind her. Arnold remained in her bedroom, hunting the spiders that remained. He couldn't believe how many of them he'd killed already. There must have been a nest in the room, freshly hatched. He wondered if the spiders were poisonous or not, and decided he should catch one alive to show someone just in case.

While he did that in the bedroom, Tara savagely scraped at herself in the shower, overflowing her hands with shampoo to run through her hair in hope that the chemicals would kill any spiders hiding there. Several fell into the drain during her stay, dead or dying. She didn't know how she could ever leave the bathroom feeling clean. She was twitching all over, as if the bastards were still on her. At last, she closed the drain and allowed the tub to fill. She then filled it with body wash and dunked her head under water until she was numb, and scratched at her scalp with her fingernails.

More than thirty minutes had passed before she got out of the tub to dry off. When she did emerge from the bathroom, trembling in shock and disgust, her father emerged from her bedroom to tell her what he'd done.

"I caught one to make sure it isn't poisonous," he said. "And killed the rest. I think you have a nest in there or something. Those spiders were hatchlings. Maybe they aren't poisonous that young. I don't know. But I'll find out." He paused and looked back over his shoulder at the room before continuing. "I think it's best if you don't sleep in there tonight. I cleaned up their guts as best as I could, and sprayed the hell out of the room with that poison your mother keeps in the closet. Hell, that might be reason enough not to sleep there overnight, because it might not be the best stuff to be breathing."

"I'm not going anywhere near the fucking room tonight," Tara said, forgetting to edit out her language.

Instead of getting on Tara about it, her father said, "I wouldn't if I were you. I'll try to figure out a better way to clean it out tomorrow. Maybe call over an exterminator while I'm at it. We don't need any more nests in this place."

Tara nodded and shivered within the towel wrapped around her.

"You think you got them all off you?" her father asked.

Tara shook harder in response. "Please, just stop talking about them."

"Sorry. You can sleep on the couch in the living room.

Have a sleepover with the TV or whatever."

"Thanks."

Her father turned away from her and headed toward his own room. Tara considered grabbing clothes from her dresser, but thought better of it. Right now, she wanted that room to burn, along with everything inside it. So, she headed downstairs with the towel and found clothing in the laundry room to wear.

In the morning, Tara forced herself to drink a cup of coffee. She hadn't slept for more than a few minutes at a time after the spider incident. Every time she drifted into dreams, spiders would invade them, hungry for her eyes. She was exhausted.

As she hovered by the sink with her mug of coffee, she felt the uneasy suspicion that someone was watching her. She looked around the room, assuming it was her father. But the downstairs level was empty and quiet.

She turned to the window and looked outside. There at the treeline was the same young woman she'd spotted several nights earlier in the rain, only this time she wasn't naked. Instead, she wore a crimson cloak and hood.

"What the fuck?" Tara mumbled, lowering her coffee and leaning over the sink for a closer look.

The girl met her gaze before turning away and disappearing into the woods.

Tara raced into the laundry room to find a pair of socks and dry shoes to wear. Once she had them on, she hurried outside and looked for the girl's tracks in the damp soil. Though there were some at the treeline, they were impossible to see through the woods. Leaves littered the ground, as did puddles of water and mud. Tara wasn't a tracker by any means, and lost her way after a few seconds.

"Damn it!"

She wanted to keep looking, but thought of her father waking up to find her missing. So, she returned to the house, wrote him a note saying she was taking a morning walk, and grabbed the walkie-talkie he had drying out in a bag of rice. She didn't know if it worked, but she hardly cared either way. She was bringing it mostly for show.

Back in the woods, she entered the trees from where she'd spotted the girl and continued straight. She hoped her spy hadn't taken a winding path to the house.

In an unusual amount of time, she stepped out of the trees and onto the rock surrounding the waterfall and its pool. Confused, Tara looked back over her shoulder and wondered how long she'd been walking. It seemed like she'd only left the yard a minute ago. The waterfall shouldn't have been this close at all. It made no sense geographically either. The mountain didn't rise this close to her house.

"What is going on?" she asked herself aloud.

"Sorry, I did that."

Tara startled and turned toward the waterfall. Sitting beside it with a small fire at her feet was the cloaked woman. She had a skillet of sizzling eggs held over the fire, and her hood was now pulled back to reveal her tempting red hair. She looked up at Tara and smiled.

"You hungry?" she asked.

Tara took several steps in her direction. "Who are you?"

"My name is Ardere."

"Ardere?"

The girl nodded and moved her gaze back onto the eggs. She shuffled the skillet over the fire a moment longer before pulling them back to rest atop the rocks surrounding her.

"Why are you out here?" Tara asked, studying her.

"I've been out here for a month or so," the girl told her. "I hadn't realized a new family had moved into the house."

"Did you used to...squat there or something?"

The girl laughed and shook her head. "No. I have kept my distance for the most part."

"Why were you watching me the other night?"

"That's not the only time I've watched you." The girl turned to produce a stone plate from behind her, and shook the eggs out of the skillet onto it. "Here," she said, holding out the plate to Tara.

"No, that's okay."

"Suit yourself." The girl began to eat with her hands, making a mess.

"Are you homeless?" Tara asked, not sure how to better word the question.

"I suppose you might consider me homeless," the girl replied. "But I don't think of myself that way."

"Why are you out here then?"

"I live in the woods all over. I'll stay in a place for a while, then leave. I've been on a mission for years and years, but finally things are lining up."

"What things?"

"People, mostly. My girls are on a pilgrimage as we speak. But we could certainly use another helpful hand."

Tara was confused and said as much.

"There's much to learn," the girl continued. "But I don't just freely offer such knowledge."

Tara opened her mouth but found that she didn't know what she could say to Ardere that wouldn't sound offensive.

The girl finished her eggs, cleaned her lips, chin, and

hands in the pool, then stood. Water glistened around her mouth, and Tara sensed a strange arousal bubbling inside her.

"Follow me," the girl told her, turning toward the waterfall.

Tara did as she was told, though she didn't understand why. Something about Ardere was luring her away from safety, she felt, but she couldn't stop herself. She felt propelled—no, *compelled*, to follow the girl and see whatever it was she wanted to show Tara.

They entered the cave from the sight, hugging the wall to avoid getting soaked by the waterfall. Inside, several candles had been placed along the walls to light the space. Tara observed the drawings she'd seen before, and noticed they'd multiplied in scale—there were more eyes now and more people worshiping from the woods beneath them.

"What is all this?" she asked the girl. "I've found eyes carved into trees also."

The girl turned to face her, several feet between them.

This close, Tara couldn't help but lust after Ardere's beauty. What was this unnatural possession she felt washing over her? It was as if the girl herself was intoxicating and...magic? That couldn't be it, but Tara thought the word nevertheless.

"The Eye of Eyes is my King. The Higher Power. These eyes in the sky you see here are his watchmen, you could say."

"I have no idea what you're talking about," Tara admitted.

"Join me and I can teach you everything."

"Join you?"

"As I've said, the Others are on a pilgrimage at this time, but I can bring you up to speed while they're away."

The girl held out a hand for Tara to take. It was scarred all over, as if it had been cut many times. Uneasy, Tara looked at it, though she felt an energy surge down her arm, attempting to lift it. Scared of the feeling, Tara took two steps back from the woman and shook her head. "What the hell is going on? I feel...st–strange."

Ardere smiled in a way that made Tara shiver. As she lowered her hand, she said, "Have you seen any of the eyes yet?"

Tara thought of her waking nightmare from two nights earlier, the one with the fiery eyeball that launched itself down her throat. "N–no," she lied.

The girl's eyes narrowed, but for less than a second.

"I, uh, have to go," Tara said, moving toward the exit. "My father is going to wonder where I am."

"Isn't that why you called that device on your belt?" the girl asked.

Tara looked down at the walkie-talkie, having completely forgotten about it. "Yes, but it isn't working," she said.

The girl nodded, watching her.

As Tara turned away and hurried outside, she heard Ardere say, "Thank you for letting me use your bathroom the other night."

She didn't tell her father. How could she?

She spent the rest of the morning in the living room on the couch, drawing and reading. More than once, she lost herself in a trance, only to find herself sketching eyes and Ardere all over her pad. Scared by this new, obsessive development, she tore out the pages and crumpled them into balls at the foot of the couch to be thrown away later. Who the hell was that girl? And what mission was she referring to? She said years had gone by, but she looked to be in her early twenties, if even in her twenties. It didn't make sense. She must have grown up in a cult or something. Maybe she was one of those crazy mountain people you read about in horror stories.

And yet, she was beautiful, a hypnotic attractiveness.

Tara cursed herself for thinking such things and decided to check in on her father. He was in his office painting as usual.

"What's up, kiddo?" he asked as she stepped inside.

"I don't know. Just bored, I guess."

"I have an exterminator coming this afternoon," he told her.

"That's good."

"You haven't seen any more of the damn things, have you?"

She shook her head.

"Good, good. Why don't you take your bike into town for a while?"

"Yeah, maybe."

Her father's gaze narrowed. "Is everything okay?"

"Yeah. Just...bored."

He didn't believe her, but nodded anyway. "Let me know if you need any money to get lunch or anything," he said, turning back to his painting.

"Okay, thanks."

Tara left the office, not sure where to go. Did she have the energy or interest to bike into town? She didn't think so. Not alone, at least. She was tempted to call Belle, even if it was to just talk for a minute and nothing more, but restrained herself from picking up the phone. She didn't know much about Belle's parents and didn't want to annoy them by calling. She'd dealt with some rude parents in the past, and therefore never made the first move to call someone as a result.

Veni ad me...

Tara nearly jumped out of her skin. She looked around herself to find who was talking, but there was no one there. Her father was the only other person home, and he was still in his office. Not only that, his voice wasn't soft or pleasant like the one she'd just heard. Whoever had spoken had a voice that was both feminine and...

Enchanting?

Veni ad me...

There it was again. Was Tara hearing it from inside her head? She searched the house for anyone else, but there was only her father in his office. Whenever she walked by, he would turn and wait for her to enter. But she never did. If he was curious about her pacing, he kept it to himself by returning to his work.

Tara determined the voice was without a body. She didn't understand how that could be, but the past week had been strange in other ways, as well. The nightmares, the spiders, the muddy footprints that vanished on their own...

And Ardere. The girl in the woods living in a secret cave behind a waterfall that seemed to change locations as it pleased.

"I'm losing my fucking mind," Tara told herself, heading outside to clear her head. But before she could enter the woods and find her trail, she stopped herself to reconsider.

If Ardere was out there, they might run into each other

again. And Tara wasn't ready for that. Not just yet.

So, she went to the shed to fetch her bicycle.

I guess I'm going into town, after all, she decided.

Saturday night was even worse than the Night of Spiders, as she'd come to think of it. The voice in her head had started talking more and more throughout the day, to the point that it was somehow overlapping itself. There were more phrases than before, all of them Latin or Italian—she wasn't sure which, and also wasn't sure how much they even differed. But she'd recognized a few words over the course of the day, including *exitium*, which translated to "destruction". Even without understanding the rest, she began to worry.

The voice wasn't the only difficult part of her night. She was also having regular hallucinations. There were eyes on her all the time, peering at her around corners and in reflections. Even in the darkness, they would blink and stare. Whenever she neared sleep, she'd feel vines wrapping around her ankles, eager to drag her out the window and to the woods. She fought these hallucinations and screamed so often that her father suggested they go to the hospital to figure out what was wrong.

"You must have a dangerous fever," he told her, "for you to be seeing and hearing things that aren't here. I'm really worried, Tara! We should go. Please."

But she fought him to stay home without being able to explain why. Maybe she worried somehow would call her possessed and order an exorcist. Or perhaps worse, someone would deem her mentally unstable and put her in an asylum.

It took several sleeping pills to put her to sleep, and by then it was after three a.m.

It was nearing noon on Sunday when Arnold Wilkins shook his daughter awake.

"Wha...what is it?" she slurred, blinking against the light breaking through her curtains.

"The phone rang for you, sweetie. It was Belle," he told her.

Tara sat up and clapped her cheeks to wake up. "Right now? She's on the phone?"

"Not anymore. I spoke with her, though."

"What did she say?"

"First things first," her father said, watching her with a furrowed brow. "How are you feeling?"

Tara considered this by scanning the room for anything that didn't belong. Everything appeared normal enough, and there were no voices speaking Latin inside her head.

"I feel...fine," she said with a shrug and smile. "Really."

Her father placed the back of his hand against her forehead, then felt the back of her neck. "You're not hot," he said.

"What did Belle want?" Tara asked again, eager for good news to help save the weekend for her.

"I'm not sure. I told her you were sleeping in late, and she asked for you to call her back."

Tara threw back the covers and climbed out of bed. "I'll call her back now!"

"Wait, wait," her father said, taking her by the shoulders. "Are you *sure* you're okay? Last night was kind of scary. You really freaked me out."

"I feel fine, Dad. Really."

"Have you, uh, noticed any spider bites on you since

that night?"

She shook her head. "No, why?"

"I thought maybe yesterday's craziness could be a reaction to a bite."

"I haven't noticed anything," she said, "but that does make me wonder. I'll take a thorough look in the shower."

"Good. Okay. Go call your friend back."

Tara hurried downstairs and into the kitchen. She wasted no time dialing Belle and cradling the phone tight to her ear. When an unfamiliar man answered the call, she began to panic, her anxiety getting the best of her. "Oh, uh, hi. This is, uh, Tara. From school. Is Belle there?"

"Yeah. Just a minute," the voice said. The phone was set down on something hard with a clicking sound.

Tara waited by pacing about the kitchen and wrapping the phone cord around her midsection as she turned in circles until she was dizzy.

"Hello?"

"Belle?"

"Tara?"

"Yes!"

Belle laughed. "You sound alert. I guess sleeping in until lunch does you good."

"I had a rough night. It was close to four before I even got to sleep, I think."

"Oh, that sucks."

"Dad said you called for me."

"Well, I certainly didn't call for him."

"I don't blame you."

Both girls giggled.

"I was wondering if you wanted to get lunch," Belle said. "I'm feeling much better now."

"Yes! Yes, yes, yes."

"Great. How about Ryan's? Do you know where that is?"

"The burger joint by the bookstore?"

"That's the one."

"Sure. What time?"

"I'm getting hungry now if you're available," she said, smiling through her voice.

"Uh, let me see... I can be there in like forty-five minutes. I need to shower and get dressed and bike over there. Is that okay?"

"Yeah, that works. I'll see you there!"

"Okay!"

Tara hung up the phone and hurried up to the bathroom, almost knocking her father over as she passed him on the stairs.

"Woah, what's going on?" he called after her.

"I'm going to meet Belle for lunch."

"Be safe!" he yelled from downstairs as she undressed next to the shower.

Though Tara was in a hurry, she checked herself for bites as best she could before getting under the spray of hot water. She found nothing but considered the validity of her father's hypothesis. Maybe she was having a reaction. The bite could be located somewhere on her scalp, beneath her hair. Or even in an awkward location along her back. She figured a bite should itch but they didn't even know what kind of spider had hatched in her bedroom. Her father had shown the exterminator the one he'd captured, but the guy didn't recognize it.

After her shower, Tara toweled off fast and got dressed. She tortured herself in the mirror before forcing herself outside to the shed—she no longer had time to continue fucking around with her looks. Belle was waiting.

She rode fast into town, working her legs harder than she had since running track for her previous high school. Her calves and thighs were burning by the time she reached Ryan's at 12:30. She found Belle already inside, sitting in a booth facing the entrance. She almost jumped out of her seat when Tara stepped inside.

She's just as happy to see you, Tara told herself. *This is good. She must like you, too.*

"Hey, Belle," she said on approach, a shy brush of the hair behind her ear.

"It feels like it's been ages," her friend said, hugging her.

Tara felt the pit of her stomach warm and her breath hitch in her chest. "It does."

Belle pulled away and said, "Well, I guess we should order something and then we can sit."

"Oh, right. Duh."

They headed to the counter and placed their order. When Belle tried paying, Belle pushed her hand away and handled it instead. As they waited at the corner of the counter for their food, Tara asked Belle how she was feeling.

"I'm still a little run down, but my throat is only a little scratchy. I should be at school tomorrow. I can't keep missing."

"Well, I think I might have scared off Kia, at least."

"Really? What happened?"

"Thursday, she hit me when we got off the bus and—"

"Wait, what? She *hit* you?"

"Yeah, but I was like *possessed* or something, like totally pissed when she did. I snapped and told her I'd tear her apart if she did it again."

Belle's eyes widened. "Whaaaaa... Really?"

"Yeah. I think I also called her a cunt."

"*Holy shit.*"

Their food arrived at the counter then. They took the trays over to a booth and sat down—Belle was eager to hear more about the Kia confrontation.

"What did she do after you said all that?"

"She looked shocked. I hurried home but...I felt *good*."

"And Friday?"

"She avoided me. And during the walk home, I even yelled at her to keep walking or something."

"None of this sounds like you."

"Because it's not! Seriously, I have no idea what was coming over me. Both times, I felt this crazy energy swelling up inside me. I'm lucky I didn't jump on her back and start pulling out her hair or something."

"Damn, girl. Good to know you're on my side," Belle said, laughing.

Tara straightened as she took a drink from her soda, and contemplated telling Belle what else had been going on with her and the girl in the woods. She was going back and forth with herself on the subject—just as she had during the bike ride into town—when Belle took notice of her change.

"What's wrong? You've tensed up."

Tara smiled at her, pleased that Belle could see through her so easily. It made her feel truly noticed by her friend that she wanted more from down the road.

"There's been more going on," she admitted.

"Like what? I only missed two days!"

"Not with school. Outside of school."

"Oh. Is everything alright?"

Tara looked away from Belle as she thought things

through. "I've been seeing and hearing things this weekend."

"Like what?"

"Someone speaking Latin in my head. And...there was the night I woke up covered in a hundred baby spiders."

"Wait, *what*?" Belle squirmed in her seat, dropping her burger onto the tray. "Spiders?"

"Yeah. And I didn't imagine them like some of the other stuff. My dad had to come rescue me. A nest had hatched or something in my room."

"Holy shit..."

"Yeah, I nearly passed out from it."

"What else have you seen?"

"Crazy things... Like eyes. Everywhere."

"Disembodied?"

"Yeah. And it all started after I found this cave in the woods."

"What cave?"

"It's behind this waterfall behind my house. But I don't know the location exactly. It always seems to change."

Belle eyed her in a way that made Tara uncomfortable. Was she losing her? She didn't want to scare Belle away from her.

"Forget it," she said. "It's crazy, I know. I think...um... I think it's just my waking nightmares returning. I had them a lot as a toddler, my parents have told me."

"What's that?"

"I guess it's like sleepwalking. I'd be awake and moving around, talking, eyes open. But I'd be dreaming and unable to see or hear my parents as they tried to calm me down."

"Jesus."

"They said I did it for like two years. I woke them up a lot during that time."

For a minute, they ate in silence before moving onto other conversations. Their lunch stretched on for an hour before Belle told her she wanted to see the waterfall. Though Tara was a little worried they'd run into Ardere there—assuming the girl was real and not one of her hallucinations—but then Belle shocked her by leaning across the table and kissing her on the lips. Though it was quick, there was a force to it that suggested physical interest in more. Tara's mouth hung open after as she stared at Belle, wondering whether or not she'd imagine the kiss.

"Did you just—"

Belle nodded, her cheeks blooming red.

Tara swallowed and nodded back. "Okay. Let's go to my house."

Belle jumped out of the booth as Tara quickly threw their trash together on one tray. "Right behind you!"

They biked side by side as often as they could. The town was small and pretty quiet, so they were able to spread out on the road multiple times during the ride. When they reached Tara's house fifteen minutes later, they jumped off their bikes and allowed them to crash into one another along the side of the driveway.

"So, this is it," Tara said, a little out of breath.

"Cute. I love that you're surrounded by the woods. Nice and private."

"I need the woods nearby," Tara admitted. "It's how I reset."

"What do you mean?"

"When I'm overwhelmed by things or upset, going into nature really helps me get my head back on straight."

"Oh, I get that. My parents and I used to hike a lot together. But now we're not around each other all that much anymore."

"Before we do anything, I think I should introduce you to my dad," Tara said, heading toward the house. "He'd be pissed if I didn't."

"What about your mom?"

"She's away for a couple days for work."

Tara led her inside and called for her father, though she assumed he was in the office as usual. He replied from down the hall, and they followed his voice. When they stepped into his office space, they found him painting a dark forest across a large canvas, the biggest Tara had seen him use in months.

"Oh, we have company," he said, smiling upon seeing Belle hiding behind Tara in the doorway. "You must be Belle."

She nodded shyly. "Hello."

"This is my dad, Arnold," Tara said.

"You can call me *Mr. Wilkins*," her father told Belle, dropping his smile. But a second later, he grinned again, laughing. "Nah, I'm just kidding. Arnold is fine."

"We're going to hang out for a bit," Tara told him. "Probably go out to the woods for a walk."

"Take the radio. I still don't know if it works, though. Test it out for me and let me know if I need to replace it already."

Tara agreed and led Belle into the kitchen to find the rice bag with the walkie-talkie inside it. When she took it out, she switched it on. The speaker crackled in response. "I guess it's working," she said to Belle with a shrug as she clipped it to the side of her belt.

They returned outside after getting drinks of water, and headed toward the woods.

"How far does this go?" Belle asked her.

"No idea. At least a few miles, I think. We're at the base of a mountain."

"Have you carved out any trails yet?"

"The previous owners made several."

"Are we going to the waterfall?"

"If I can find it."

Belle bumped into her for second. Tara wasn't sure if it was an accident or not, but she blushed nonetheless.

"You don't know where it is?" Belle asked.

"No, that's part of the strange stuff that's been happening..."

"What do you mean?"

"It seems to change locations in the woods," Tara explained. "I know that sounds crazy, but I always stumble upon it by accident, and one of the times it was only shortly after entering the woods. Which makes no sense because it was much further out the other two times."

"Are you sure it was the same waterfall each time?"

"Yeah. The cave was there every time."

"And what makes the cave so special?"

"Um..."

Belle gave her a sideways look as they walked through the trees. "What is it?"

"The cave is full of drawings."

"Ooo, like ancient stuff?"

"No. There's a...um... A girl lives out here."

Belle stopped. Tara walked several more steps before pausing to turn around.

"A girl is living out here?" Belle asked her.

"That's what she told me."

"Like, camping?"

"In the cave, I guess."

"Oh, that is so fucking weird."

Tara nodded.

"So, you've met her? Is she crazy? Dangerous?"

"I don't know. She said some strange stuff to me, but she didn't *act* crazy."

Belle bridged the gap between them and they started walking once more. "Well...okay. Let's find this waterfall."

They searched for an hour before giving up. As they left the woods and headed back toward the house, Belle asked, "Is it possible the waterfall was another hallucination?"

"I guess so," Tara mumbled. She was angry and embarrassed.

As if sensing this, Belle took her hand and squeezed it as they approached their discarded bikes. "It's okay," Belle said. "Maybe your dad was onto something about the spider bite. You think you'll go to the doctor? Maybe have them draw blood or something?"

"I don't know. Maybe." She felt shut down, and in front of Belle, no less. Tara wanted to scurry under her bed covers and hide.

Belle bent over to pick up her bike. "I'll see you at school tomorrow?"

Tara nodded.

Belle positioned herself close to Tara and said, "I enjoyed getting some time with you," she said. "You know, outside of school."

With a weak smile, Tara kept her gaze to the side, scared to meet Belle's eyes. But Belle was far more assertive than she, and placed a hand against Tara's cheek to turn her face. Tara swallowed as her heart began to race.

"Hey," Belle said.

Tara met her gaze.

Belle leaned in and kissed her deeply. Tara felt like she was on fire and levitating. When Belle pulled away slowly, Tara's eyes were still shut, her mouth still open a little.

"See you tomorrow," Belle said, climbing onto her bike and taking off down the driveway.

Tara watched her go, breathless for several minutes. Once she'd collected herself enough to walk, she headed into the house to find her father. When she entered his office to tell him Belle had gone home, she almost fell backwards in shock.

His painting on the large canvas now featured a dozen eyes of various sizes littering the night sky. Tara tried to scream but it caught in her throat as she stumbled against the doorway. Her father turned in his chair to look at her and said, "What's wrong?"

"Wh—"

"You don't like it?"

Tara squeezed her eyes shut, counted to three with slow breaths, and then looked at the painting again. The eyes were no longer there.

"Thank god," she whispered.

Her father watched her close, concerned. "What's going on, sweetie? Are you hallucinating again?"

She licked her lips and shrugged. "I'm b–better now."

He nodded, his eyes glued to her face. "Why don't you send Belle home and get some rest?"

"She actually just left."

"That's probably for the best. Take some, I don't know, allergy medicine or something and lie down for a bit. I know you've only been up a couple hours, but you're really making me worry."

"Belle said I should get blood drawn. To test your spider bite theory," Tara offered, still trying to calm herself. The tremors in her fingers were still ringing.

"That might not be such a bad idea. I'll call the doctor in the morning and see what we can set up."

"What about school?"

"I can take you out for an hour," he told her. "And if they raise a fuss, they can fuck themselves."

Tara smiled and turned away from her father. "I guess I'll go lie down then."

"Good."

Once upstairs in her room, she climbed under her blankets and embraced the darkness beneath them. Her heart began to steady in rhythm a few minutes later. Tara smiled to herself and relaxed atop the bed, curling onto her side and getting comfortable. She was almost asleep when she felt something watching her. She opened her eyes slowly and saw only darkness.

At first.

Then an eye blinked back at her in the black.

Monday morning, Tara looked a mess. After going to bed Sunday afternoon, she'd struggled with waking nightmares and hallucinations all through the day and night. Her eyes were red from rubbing them and her hair was in knots. She didn't even try to make herself presentable for school—she was just too tired and haunted to care.

When Belle saw her in between classes, she asked what was going on.

"It got so much worse after seeing you yesterday." Tara

yawned as she fumbled with her books at her locker.

"How so?"

"I couldn't get any sleep without a nightmare. I just kept seeing things and... I don't even know if this conversation is actually happening or not. I'm in a daze."

"Jesus, Tara. Maybe you should go home."

"My dad is supposed to get me at some point to take me to the doctor, like you suggested."

"Good. Just hang in there until it arrives. Take it easy."

"I'm trying."

Later, in her fourth class, Tara hit a wall. Her teacher had given a stack of assignments to the front row to pass around the class. When it came time for Tara to pick a paper and pass it along, her head was down on the desk and she was oblivious. The student passing her the stack—a guy from the wrestling team—saw this and dropped the papers onto her head. As they scattered, she looked up, zeroed in on him and his laughing friends, and screamed for him to "Fuck the hell off." The teacher kicked her out of class to go see the principal.

But she didn't go to the office. Instead, she walked right out the front doors, through the parking lot, and to the road. She intended on walking home regardless of the consequences. As for her father picking her up, she'd forgotten—she wasn't even aware of the world around her at this point. Every time she directed her gaze to anything specific, she would see an eye where it didn't belong. The Stop signs blinked at her, as did the trees and the hoods of passing cars. She couldn't escape them. She was being watched no matter where she turned.

Iungere nobis...
...aut pascere caelum.

"Shut up," she groaned, clapping her hands over her ears as she stumbled down the road. "Shut up, shut up, shut up."

It felt like her brain was on fire. On occasion, a wave of heat would wash over her entire body, making her sick. She shook and twitched and lacked control of herself. It was as if she was moving on autopilot.

Time had also changed for her. It seemed she was leaping forward every time she blinked or lifted her head to inspect her surroundings. She soon found herself in the woods behind her house, though she should have still been several miles away. When she looked down at herself, she saw her legs were trembling. They ached. The soles of her feet were blistered and stinging. The back of her neck and arms were red with sunburn.

"How did I get here?" she asked herself. *This doesn't make any sense.*

"Well, look at you."

Tara blinked again and looked up from her shuffling feet. She was stepping onto the rocks surrounding the waterfall. Ardere was standing by the pool, watching her.

"You," Tara said, sleepy.

"Me. I have to say, Tara—you don't look so good."

"What do you want, Ardere?"

"Oh, good. You remember my name. Effects can vary with this spell, I'll admit. Some girls completely lose their fucking minds." The girl laughed and approached Tara, removing her cloak as she neared. "Have you reconsidered my offer? The girls will be back any day now. I'm sure they'd love a new recruit."

"I don't understand," Tara told her. "I don't understand what is going on. Who you are. What you want."

"The Eye of Eyes provides. We are preparing for the end of the world, I suppose you could say. Only it won't be the end for us. Far from it."

Tara was standing still but wavering back and forth as if she might fall any second. "You're crazy."

"Let me try something else," the girl said, producing an ancient knife from her cloak and splitting open the palm of her hand. Before Tara couldn't even think to act, the girl placed her bloodied palm against Tara's chest and whispered something in an unfamiliar language. It could have been Latin or something even older.

"What are you doing?" Tara asked. Suddenly, she was flooded with images she couldn't explain. Marching trees. A blackened sky filled with eyes. Raging fires. Blood and gore. A monstrous creature that stood tall and white. Then galaxies of stars and planets bursting like bombs, one by one until an all-consuming, blinding light struck Tara so hard that she was thrown backwards onto the rocks.

"How about now?" Ardere asked, standing over. "Do you believe me now?"

Scared, Tara picked herself up from the ground and ran into the woods, away from the waterfall.

Ardere called after her in a sing-songy voice, "If you do not choose us, that nasty fever in your brain will only get worse."

Spilling out of the trees, Tara ran into her backyard. She scrambled across the grass, tripping over her feet a few times before reaching the back door and trying to open it. But it was locked and she didn't have any of her things with her. She must have left it all at school in the classroom.

"Shit!"

She began to pound on the door, unaware that her

father had left to pick her up from school. She couldn't take it anymore—her brain was burning and the voices were so constant and overlapping that she couldn't understand a word of them anymore. She began to shoulder the door harder and harder until the lock broke and she fell inside. Kicking the door shut behind her, she crawled into the kitchen crying.

She lifted herself up against the island counter and found herself a knife.

She needed to make the voices stop.

Arnold Wilkins was furious. Not only did the school tell him Tara had dismissed herself without a word to anyone, but she'd first screamed obscenities during class. How could she have left on foot, though? He knew she wasn't doing well, but this was taking things to another level. She was becoming violent and self-destructive. He needed to get her tested straight away, and not at the doctor's office. He needed to take her to a hospital and hope for the best.

As he drove home, he called his wife to tell her what had been happening. She said she'd be home tomorrow afternoon—it was the best she could do. Frustrated, Arnold ended the call without saying goodbye. When he pulled into the driveway, he raced down it toward the house, kicking up rocks along the way.

"Tara!" he yelled, storming into the house with his keys in hand. "Where are you?"

It didn't take long to find her. There was blood all over the kitchen floor, in circles as if Tara had been pacing. When he saw her standing over the sink with her hands held under the running faucet, he felt his heart leap into his throat.

"Tara?"

She didn't turn. Her back remained on him as he inched closer.

"Tara? Honey?"

Still nothing.

There was blood on her shoulders and arms, but he couldn't see her hands. She appeared to be washing them. Where was the blood coming from? What had she done to herself? He needed to call for an ambulance. But first, he needed to know where she was hurt...

"Tara?" He placed a hand on her shoulder and turned her.

His daughter spun in place and thrust a bloodied knife into his gut, pushing him back against the island. Now that he could see her face, he realized why she hadn't heard him—her ears were gone. Crimson threads of skin hung in their place, entwined with her sticky hair.

He couldn't feel the knife at first. But upon seeing his daughter's self-mutilation, the blade in his gut made Arnold lower his gaze and scream.

"What have you done?"

At first, it didn't seem that Tara recognized them. But then her eyes widened in shock and she stumbled backwards against the sink.

"Da–daddy?"

Arnold repeated himself as he fell to the floor, clutching the knife handle protruding from him. "What have you done?"

Tara began to sob, turning her head erratically from side to side as she looked elsewhere. Arnold watched her, confused. It seemed as if she could see things that he could not. She began screaming at the kitchen behind him, though there was nothing there he could see or hear.

"Leave him alone! Stay away from us! Stay away!"

Arnold shuddered as a cold swept over him. "Honey? Wha—what's happening? Who's here? Call 911, please..."

Tara's eyes fell on him and narrowed. Again, she didn't seem to recognize him. She took hold of the knife handle and tore the blade out of his gut. He pressed his hands against his wound as the knife came out, and fell onto his side, gasping and crying from the pain. Tara stood over him, a girl possessed. Her eyes had whitened, as if she'd gone blind.

Arnold began to plead with her as his energy ebbed from his body. "Honey, please... Call for help..."

The knife flashed through the air and planted into the side of his neck this time. He grunted, but little else. The knife stabbed into him again and again until Arnold couldn't feel anything anymore. With his face pressed against the bloodied tiled floor, he looked toward the fridge and faded into nothingness.

Two days passed. Belle had not seen Tara in school, nor had she been able to reach her by telephone. She was sick with worry. Something must have happened.

When she arrived outside Tara's house Wednesday evening, just as the sun was setting over the surrounding trees, she saw two vehicles in the driveway, both crooked as if they'd parked in a hurry.

They're home, she told herself as she leaned her bicycle against a tree. *That has to be a good thing, right?*

She sniffed the air. Something was burning in the backyard. She could see smoke in the air and smell meat. Were they having a cookout for dinner?

Belle's concern began to fade. The Wilkins family must have been celebrating Tara's recovery. Maybe they'd taken her to the hospital after all.

She rounded the vehicles and headed down the side yard to the back of the house. When she turned the corner, she found a bonfire burning with a slight crackle, its flames low and perhaps dying. In the midst of the charred wood pile were two shapes that made her freeze mid-step.

What?

She couldn't process what she was seeing. Those were bodies, weren't they? Blackened, flaking bodies with exposed skulls and jaws hanging open.

"No," Belle said aloud to herself, as if that would erase the scene before her. "No. No."

Something crashed from inside the house. Belle turned, but did not move any further into the yard. She was frozen in place, terrified.

Someone had murdered the Wilkins. Was Tara dead, too? Was the killer still inside the house, robbing them?

Before she could force herself to turn away from the house and run, the back door opened, its frame splintered around the lock. Tara stepped outside with a revolver in hand, her eyes lowered upon it. She walked several steps outside before looking up and spotting Belle at the corner, eyes wide and tears staining her cheeks.

"Belle?"

"Ta–Tara?"

For several long seconds, nobody said a word. As Belle watched Tara from afar, she realized her friend's ears were missing and that she was wearing the same clothes she'd had on Monday morning, the last she'd seen her. Only now, they were stained with blood and dirt.

"What happened to you?" Belle asked, her voice barely a whisper. Did it even matter, though? Her friend could no longer hear anything.

Tara's face crumpled upon itself and she began to sob. "I can't make it stop," she screamed, gripping the revolver tight in her hands. Her words were muffled and unclear. "They won't leave me alone! I can still hear them! I can still see them!"

Belle watched in horror as her friend paced back and forth about the backyard with her gun, tears soaking her face as she stomped her right feet.

"It must stop!"

Belle swallowed and looked toward the open door. If she could run inside and find the telephone, call the police…

Would Tara shoot her? Had Tara been the one to kill her parents?

"Why are you here?!" Tara screamed, looking at Belle now with mistrust. "You're another trick! Another fucking trick!"

Belle wanted to run—was desperate to get out of there—but her muscles were locked in place. Fear had a death grip on her and would not let go.

Tara fell to her knees and smacked her hands and the revolver against her head, where her ears used to be. "They won't shut up! That fucking girl in the woods—she did this to me! She did this to me!"

Belle looked toward the trees, felt the sudden weight of someone's gaze upon her. But there was no one else there but Tara.

"Let's… Let's get you to a hos–hospital," Belle offered, holding out a shaking hand toward her friend. "We–we can fix this. We can get you help."

Tara's eyes shot back on her. "No more tricks!" she screamed, raising the revolver and taking aim at Belle.

Finally, she found it in herself to run. Turning, she fell, and got back onto her feet. A blast of gunfire echoed around her as Tara pulled the trigger on her revolver. Belle did not stop. She made it to her bike a second later and jumped onto it. As she began to pedal down the driveway, she looked back over her shoulder.

There was someone wearing a crimson cloak stepping out of the woods toward Tara as she stumbled into the side yard with her gun still raised. Tara turned to face her, screamed, and thrust the revolver against her temple. When the dull shot echoed, Belle lost control of her bike and fell, unable to remove her eyes from Tara's collapsing form.

From the gravel, bruised and bleeding, Belle watched as the cloaked figure turned away from Tara to look in her direction instead.

The figure lowered their hood and smiled.
Veni ad me...

THE CRIMSON HIGHNESS WILL RETURN

This novelette is just one of many stories coming soon from *The Crimson Highness*, a series that preludes the events of *The Fucked* trilogy (of which *Feed the Sky* is book one). Go back more than a century to learn the story of Ardere from birth to adulthood to bloody pilgrimage.

WANT MORE FROM THE COSMIC DEVOURER OF LIFE SERIES?

The Fucked trilogy has two more forthcoming episodes.

The Crimson Highness, which tells the backstory of Ardere, is expected to officially premier with its first novella in 2026.

Show your love (or hatred) for *Feed the Sky* by leaving an honest review wherever you can!

Reviews and word of mouth are the lifeblood of the indie scene, so everything mentioning this book is very much appreciated.

Find more from Wintry Monsters Press:
www.wintrymonsterspress.com

ALSO AVAILABLE NOW
THE TOLL COMES DUE

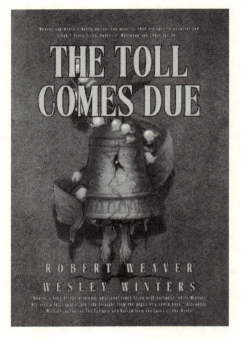

"Weaver and Winters deftly deliver two novellas that are equally powerful and bleak."
Steve Stred, award-nominated author of *Mastodon* and *Churn the Soil*

"Weaver's hand brings a solemn, emotional touch laced with darkness, while Winters' delivers a fast, aggressive ride straight from the pages of a comic book."
Alexander Michael, author of *The Galleria* and *Called from the Cares of the World*

"The Toll Comes Due pairs two authors with distinct and powerfully passionate styles who become, here, a combined force of Gothic noir storytelling, rivalling the masters of the genre with a delightful offering of cinematic, dangerous and adrenaline-fueled prose. Weaver's The Last Chime is a perfectly dark exploration of monstrosity that ramps up with an electric and growing finality, and Winters' Going Sideways does just that, pulling the reader frantically in one direction before wheeling off in another."
Derek Heath, author of *Marsh Lights* and *Empire of Cold*

Robert Weaver, author of the Occult Britain series, and Wesley Winters, author of *Nobody's Savior*, have teamed up for a themed crime fiction split about facing oneself and the person we have become versus who we still can be.

The Last Chime by Robert Weaver

They're on the run, hiding from the police in a remote and forgotten farmhouse. They are not alone. There's a man in a church bell nearby, a man of legend and supposed fiction. Will he be their savior or destroyer?

Going Sideways by Wesley Winters

When brothers Pip and Bet accept a job to kidnap a child from the playground, they quickly learn the "simple" assignment is far more complicated and dangerous than they'd been led to believe. Not only is the child the District Attorney 's offspring, but their employer is one of the most feared and monstrous gangsters in the city.

GET IT IN PAPERBACK, HARDCOVER, & EBOOK FORMATS

ALSO AVAILABLE NOW
NOBODY'S SAVIOR

"Achingly intimate, lushly haunting, cuttingly timely, with each tale as elegantly woven as a black widow's web, *Nobody's Savior* is the ghost of hope inside a broken heart. A generous offering of variety, from stories cut from the same family quilt as *Hereditary* for their warped portraitures of the warmly homey turned surreal and strange, to updated takes on the darkly familiar such as literal monsters under the bed, the future frights that artificial intelligence is pushing at us with both hands, minivan-swallowing roadside portals, and the fork-tailed demon of bigotry, this collection will shiver readers' spines as much as it puts them through the emotional thresher. Recommended for the weary--and aren't we all?--but also the down-but-not-out, for a golden gem of daring to dream for a better tomorrow still glows deep in Winters' worlds, under all the blood and choking black dust of the apocalypse. A brilliant assemblage of modern short-form horror."
Andrew Post, author of *Chop Shop* and *Milk Teeth*

"Grab your flashlight and drape that sheet over your head. These are horrifically decadent tales meant to be read on a moonless, blustery night. Winters delivers the goods."
Hunter Shea, author of *Combustible* and *Creature*

Darkness can be found all around us and inside us. It surrounds those we call friends and family. Some of it is obvious, like a monster under your child's bed or a mysterious woman stalking you from the woods. Some of it is hidden, like in the depths of our broken hearts or in the community that pretends to embrace us. Sometimes, the darkness falls from above and blankets the world you know in red.

Nobody's Savior is a selection of stories about grief, self-destruction, hopelessness, and the accompanying dread.

In "Ghosts of Hessington Hills," Tye Cameron and his husband move to a college town in Virginia to start over but they quickly become targeted by a homophobic group of harassers.

In "The Antidote," the Nano Teeth Virus has killed millions. Those that survived now reside in small communities without federal government. A group calling themselves The Antidote are traveling from refuge to refuge with a message, one that comes with shocking violence.

In "Clouds of Red," something is falling from the clouds that clumps together and fills your lungs until you can no longer breathe. Mark hurries to his sister's house to hide out with her and his secret lover, her husband, as the world around them quickly comes crashing down.

These horrific stories and more await in the debut collection from Wesley Winters!

GET IT IN PAPERBACK & EBOOK FORMATS

ALSO AVAILABLE NOW
FROM THE FLOOD

I knew I was sick for years before my transformation, but I never found help for it. There was a time I wondered about my brain and why it did the things it did. I played the guessing game we all do at one point or another and made assumptions followed by accusations. In the end, it didn't matter, though. Because last year, I started eating the dead things my cat brought home to me.

Excerpt from "Staring Down the No-Man"

From the Flood is the second collection of stories and poetry from Wesley Winters. It features themes of distress and hopeless that soak through the pages, making them heavy. Where *Nobody's Savior* favored tech-horror and disaster, *From the Flood* leans heavily on avoidance and escapism.

A lighthouse overlooks a beach where severed limbs were once discarded by a serial killer...

A sinkhole opens up in the middle of a dark road as the sky overhead begins to shimmer...

An antique doll wants nothing more than to return to its owner...

A yellow house is for sale at an unbelievable price, but it comes with odd stipulations from the family...

A bullied teenager is granted power that corrupts them as much as it protects them...

A grotesque transformation begins with the eating of dead things...

A couple struggles to keep their relationship alive in the midst of the zombie apocalypse as neighbor after neighbor begins to vanish...

These stories and more await you in Wesley Winters' latest collection.

GET IT IN PAPERBACK & EBOOK FORMATS

ABOUT THE AUTHOR

Wesley Winters first entered the independent publishing scene in 2019 as Aiden Merchant with two story collections released several months apart. He went on to write more than a hundred stories and poems—including the crime fiction novella *Crossing Red* and the extreme collection *Horrific Holidays*—before breaking away from Merchant to try other things under the guise of several unknown aliases.

Wesley Winters was first introduced in 2023 in the anthologies *HorrorScope: Volume 2* and *That Old House: The Bathroom (Part 2)* before *Nobody's Savior* reached publication in 2024 with Slashic Horror Press. That collection was followed a year later by *Feed the Sky*, the first entry in an extreme horror trilogy called *The Fucked*, as well as another collection of horror fiction and poetry called *From the Flood*. Several months later, he decided to bring all his work together under the Winters' name, as he was no longer concerned with using different aliases to publish his varied fiction and nonfiction projects.

Winters was born at the tail end of the 80s and grew up in the 90s alongside the Chesapeake Bay. He first started writing professionally as a music journalist, appearing in a variety of international magazines, before then jumping into fiction a decade later. He is a married man with three children. His many personalities never cease to leave him alone, but he tries not to talk to them in public.

Made in the USA
Columbia, SC
08 July 2025